Journey
Back to the Roots

Sujay Chatterjee

ISBN 979-8-89446-668-2

Sarva mangalya mangalye shive sarvartha sadhike

Sharanye trambake gauri narayani namastute

You are the most auspicious of all auspicious !!!

Oh, beloved of lord shiva you are the giver of wealth of all kinds !

We take your refuge, oh three eyed goddess,

Accept our salutation, Oh Narayani

Contents

Contents

Foreword

I met Sujay for the first time in June 2024 in the Danish city of Aarhus which I was visiting to celebrate the International Day of Yoga celebrations being organized by the local Indian community. Having arrived recently in Denmark to assume charge as Ambassador, this was my first visit to any city out of Copenhagen. I was pleasantly surprised to find a very vibrant Indian community not only in the capital city of Denmark but even in other corners of the country.

Today the Indian community numbers about twenty thousand in Denmark. Sujay is one among them of these remarkable Indians who have ventured out of India and with their hard work, intellect and sincerity established themselves successfully in these foreign lands, contributing to the economy of Denmark, respecting the local culture and trying to integrate. Their presence strengthens the popular aspect of India-Denmark friendship and diplomatic relations.

The yearning of the Indian diaspora abroad for India, their memories of their lived culture and languages from their native regions of India and their efforts to remain connected with their roots is manifested in diverse ways – celebration of Indian festivals in Denmark, creating community and cultural organizations and coming together on nationals days like the Republic Day, the Independence Day, Gandhi Jayanti and other such occasions.

Sujay has gone a step ahead and written this novel which captures the whole festive mood of Durga Puja in Bengal and his native city of Kolkata. Millions of Indians celebrating Durga Puja, especially in Bengal have their own memories of this annual occasion, the enthusiasm, the fervour and devotion which surrounds it. Sujay's novel develops in a very interesting way how different characters of the story revolve around the theme of Durga Puja. Sujay not only writes but lives this experience now even in his adopted home in Denmark bringing the local Indian community to celebrate this festival. Danish friends of Sujay also join enthusiastically and marvel at the beauty of Indian culture whose glimpse they get in Denmark through the vibrant but small Indian community which has made Denmark its home. Like Sujay's kids, the children of the Indian community would also benefit from works such as those of Sujay, which span both worlds – of Denmark and India – adding to the cultural connect between the two countries in their own small ways.

I like Sujay's novel and hope that it would be rewarding for you too. My best wishes to Sujay. Hope he keeps us enthralled with more of his works to come in future.

(Manish Prabhat)
Ambassador of India in Denmark

Acknowledgements

A writer is an end product of his environment, emotions, and experiences. I am highly grateful to Maa Durga, who has filled my life with so many wonderful people that I would have to write a book separately to thank everyone.

So, I would like to pay my tribute to my parents (Pranab Kumar Chatterjee & Snigdha Chatterjee) for always encouraging me to think openly and filling my childhood with so many wonderful experiences of Durga pujo (some of which I have incorporated into this book), my parents in law (Manas Kumar Mukherjee & Sudarshana Mukherjee) for all their love and encouragement. I try to keep your daughter happy (most of the time ☺).

Thanks to my better half, Debashree Chatterjee, for bringing out the writer in me and keeping up with my many out of the box interpretations of the situations.

I would like to thank the kids of our family Misti, Dhruv, and Pakhi for turning me into a much more empathetic person, which I feel is much required quality for a writer. It is a delight to see them grow.

Lot of gratitude for Vidya Banerjee, Barnali Sengupta madam, Saurabh Suman, and Arpita Chatterjee for taking the interest to read the manuscript and give me their valuable feedback.

Few words from the Readers

This book resonates deeply with first generation NRIs as it delves into their intricate dance between multiple cultures and identities. It captures their relentless pursuit to bridge the gap between the next generation and their cultural heritage, while also grappling with their own evolving roots. Sujay's narrative gracefully encapsulates eight years of personal exploration, offering a candid glimpse into the reflections of a father navigating this journey alongside his young daughter.

Readers, particularly those who have established themselves away from their homeland, will find solace and familiarity in Sujay's narration of the story. Eagerly anticipating next installment from Sujay Chatterjee.

Rajiv Banerjee & Vidhya Variyath Banerjee
(Senior Management professional, successfully raised their children in four different countries while remaining connected to Indian roots)

Preface

This story is about reconnection with one's roots, culture, and upbringing. Joy, the protagonist of the story, hails from an Indian Bengali family and is presently settled in Denmark with his mother, wife Shree and daughter Misti. Though he belongs to a zamindar (landlord) family in Bengal, he is almost disconnected from the Bengali culture because of the preoccupations and the distance between the culture and the homeland. He is often filled with guilt that he is not giving enough exposure of Bengali culture to his daughter, and she may face an identity crisis in future.

Don't worry, this story is not about this common issue faced by most of the non-residential Indians, irrespective of their culture. This story is about a turn of events that leads Joy to return to his roots and reconnect with his culture.

It often happens with all of us that because of frequent adaptation to our surroundings and people around us, we change so much that we often forget or suppress our true selves. But that is securely preserved in some remote corner of our soft heart, waiting to resurface at an opportune moment. The joy of expressing our true selves is the joy we all long for...

Let's see for ourselves how that happens with our main character in this book... JOY.

What the 'Joy'

The alarm beeps once, and Joy swiftly moves his fingers over the mobile to switch it off. He has been dabbling in the bed for quite some time as it gets bright in Denmark around 0430 am during summer. He has the habit of waking before the alarm rings and waiting for it to ring to start the day. It has been ten years since he shifted to Denmark, so he has learned to speak Danish and has some Danish friends as well. Besides being known for its dairy products, Denmark is also known as one of the pioneers in the development of wind turbines that harness power from wind energy. Joy is working as a project manager at one of the wind turbine manufacturers.

Denmark has a population of 5.8 million, which is much less than the population of Kolkata. He lives in a town named Herning with his beloved wife Shree, daughter Misti and his mother, whom he calls Maa. Denmark is divided into five regions: Capital region, Midtjylland, Sjælland, Nordjylland and Syd Denmark, and Herning is part of Mid Jylland, which is basically central Denmark.

Herning had once been the textile capital of Denmark and this is very well reflected in the architecture as well as the lifestyle, which always has a tinge of regality clinged to it.

Joy lives in a half-timbered building constructed way back in 1960, with the roof made of red bricks in the pyramidal shape. The windows are carved out of the rooms like two eyes, when looked from outside. The floors were made of polished timber, which is more convenient to walk on during the winters, when temperature here touches -10 degrees on an odd day.

People here are obsessed with light colours, and when you visit any home in Denmark mostly, you will find the walls of the homes to be invariably white. There are hardly any high-rise buildings in Herning, and most of the houses are either one or two floors high. Each house invariably has a small garden nicely maintained with colourful floral plants, creating an ambience of the visit to a flowery paradise. Since Denmark has a very good social welfare system where your health and education expenses are covered by the government, people are less interested in saving money for the future and more interested in enjoying the present.

Joy lives in a rented tenement and if you take a property on rent then, any owner normally takes 3 months' rent as advance and deducts the money for the repairs, when you leave the house, if it is not maintained well. Something which superficially looks very correct, pricks you when you see your rented accommodation turned into completely new for the next tenant at your expense.

Since Misti has taken her painting skills to the walls of the apartment, you can see a boat rowing somewhere, a tree, a frog, a girl etc., inscribed on the wall and Joy had accepted that he is not going to get his deposit money back.

Cycling is an important part of life here and besides very few roads you will find special cycling tracks, to facilitate commuting to different places through cycles. People here like to keep pets, so much so that the rental agreement specifically mentions whether you are entitled to keep pets or not, along with permissible numbers.

You will find people here very cordial, and they greet each other with 'Hej,' which means Hi. Everything here works on schedule: trains, meetings, social gatherings and even cremations.

What the 'Joy'

Joy was denied home by an owner only because he reached to see the house 5 minutes late from the appointment time. If you have a garden in your home, then you are expected to maintain it and the owner normally appoints a caretaker who would visit your home regularly to check whether it is properly maintained or not.

Whenever Maa sees Joy tending the garden, she starts nagging him, citing past instances when she had to take up her stick to send Joy to look after their ancestral rice fields and ponds. His father, Projoy Mukherjee, was the zamindar (landlord) of Shantipur village in India and had huge quarters of land spread across the village. He would often insist that Joy should go with his assistant for a tour of the village and look after the agricultural produce from time to time; however, Joy would smartly slip out with his friends to engage in notorious activities. There were few exceptions when he would get caught by his Maa, who would then diligently send him to the fields.

In Denmark, you don't get freshwater fish like Rohu, Katla, and Elish, which are the household names in India. Normally these fish are imported from Thailand, Bangladesh, and Philippines in frozen state. By the time you buy one of such fish, you notice that the fish was packed almost two years ago.

Joy and Maa would fight for hours, discussing the variety of fishes in Denmark and India, but all these fights were tied loosely with an underscore of love and affection.

Joy always loved his Maa to be as talkative as this forever.

It's 0630 now, and Joy needs to wake up his daughter Misti and make her ready the school while Shree prepares breakfast for all.

Misti sleeps with her grandmother, whom she lovingly calls mum-mum.

Joy was ushered into the room by the visceral smell of Camphor which Maa offers Goddess Durga every morning. Goddess Durga is the representation of the feminine half of the supreme God and considered as reincarnation of Goddess Shakti.

Durga is their patrilineal goddess, and their lineage has been an ardent devotee of Goddess Durga for generations. It is to be seen what Goddess Durga has in store for them for the future.

Joy reclined to touch the feet of Maa and greeted: 'Good morning, Maa.'

Maa: God bless you beta. My sweet son. Shree is the luckiest person in this world as she has you. This dialogue remains the same all the time.

Joy then sneaks into Misti's blanket, and she understands that it's time for her to wake up.

Misti: Baba would you please stop teasing me in the morning, I can get ready even if I get up after five mins. I am having a beautiful dream, let me complete it.

Joy places his cold hand on Misti's shoulder, and she curls further into the blanket.

Joy: Misti, be like your dad. I used to be an early riser. Family members used to call me cock as I used to wake up so early.

Maa: No, you were like a hen, always found to be sitting at one place and doing nothing...as if laying an egg. You were also called monkey by many as you were very fond of eating bananas.

What the 'Joy'

Joy responds sarcastically: Thanks for your kind adjectives, Maa.

Maa: Do you know that your maternal aunt also used to call you an Owl as you were very reluctant to sleep at night.

Shree laughs from the kitchen.

Joy: Come on Misti let's get ready for the school before your mum-mum derives new animal names for your father.

Joy makes Misti brush her teeth, and then he gets ready for the office.

As Joy gets ready for the office, he notices that Misti is still not ready.

Joy: Hey Misti. What are you waiting for?

Misti was vacillating from one point to another searching for something, frantically looking below the bed or inside the almirah.

Joy: Misti, what happened?

Misti: I am not getting my socks. MAA ..., MAA, where are my socks?

Shree: Wait a minute, I am in the kitchen. I am coming in a minute.

Joy: You need not call your mum for this as your baba is enough for such small issues, where are your used socks?

Misti: There it is, I have kept it there for washing.

Joy: Bring it here fast.

Joy overturns the socks to the other side and slips it into Misti's feet.

There was a victorious smile on his face while he was doing this.

He stood up and took Misti on his lap to move into the drawing room.

Shree: Here are the socks, it was left to be folded hence was lying in the drawing room.

Misti: See here; Baba has found such a nice solution and extends her legs towards her mum.

Shree gives Joy a frowning look as she replaces the socks misti used with fresh ones.

Joy: Hurry up Misti we need to rush for school, it is getting late and please do not forget to kiss your beautiful mummy.

Shree blushes: Hmm, I am not a kid who will get lost in your appeasements.

Misti reaches towards the dining table and opens the lid of her tiffin box.

Misti: Mom, what is this? I am not going to eat these stuffed wraps.

Shree: These are not stuffed wraps; they are paratha! They are not like your Michael uncle, who changes their name once they change their country.

Michael Tripaty is a friend of Joy in Denmark who changed his name from Mahipal to Michael, as this name is very common and can be easily pronounced by the local people. He has been here for the last eight years. Joy did not change his name as it is pronounced the same here with a different meaning, 'happiness' in place of 'victory' in Bengali.

Misti: For me, these are wraps.

Shree: But why? Tomorrow, you will start calling Sabzi sushi and give Joy a corner glance, engrossed in eating the paratha.

Joy: This happened with me as well, but initially I told them that I am having Indian pancakes and subsequently I told them that Indian pancakes are called paratha in Hindi which is the national language of India and they understood.

Misti gave a million-dollar smile, which she quite often showers on everyone.

Soon, they packed their bags and set off for the day.

Joy leans to give Shree a cheek kiss, and she responds with a light pinch in the hand. This was their way of wishing 'Good day' to each other.

Misti studies in a kindergarten as here formal schooling starts from the moment you are 6 years. It's like heaven for the child as you get to play with children of your age and secondly there is no stress on formal education during this time.

Here it is believed that the first five years are the most formative years of the child and hence they invest this time on teaching their child human values like integrity, loyalty, and manners.

Small conversations in the car are always special, and Joy and Misti also used to have small chats on their way to school every day.

Joy: How was your day yesterday at school, Misti?

Misti: Yesterday we saw the actual fish, baba.

Joy: Oh. Did you go to the riverside yesterday?

Misti: No, Baba, they showed us a fish in the water, and then they cut it in front of us to show the different parts of their body.

Joy smiled and responded: Oh, that's great.

Misti: The fish which you bring for me from the supermarket is not a complete fish but just a portion of the fish.

Joy smiles again and replies: 'My sweetheart is getting more learned day by day.'

Joy was reminded of his own childhood, wherein his father Projoy Mukherjee would take him to the fish market every morning with him and used to make him identify different varieties of fishes.

People used to get surprised to see zamindar babu in the market, however Projoy Mukherjee used to consider this as his duty as a father, so that his son grows up to be a pure Bengali.

Joy was frequently asked a common question, 'Which preparation of fish do you like?'

Joy used to reply: 'Elish maach bhaat, 'which is a recipe of Hilsa fish cooked with mustard, and there used to be a laughter riot.'

Projoy Mukherjee would then move ahead holding Joy by his hand, with his parting comment 'This is called Bengali boy, he sees fish even in his dreams and people will start laughing again.'

There had been many cases when the teacher would complain to zamindar babu about the frequent absenteeism of Joy in the class, however Joy would not get scolded for this, if he is either catching fish or playing football.

Joy was feeling guilty, as Misti had never experienced those paraphernalia attached with Bengali culture, however he used to console himself by justifying himself that life is much easier and comfortable here compared to India.

What the 'Joy'

Misti: Baba, my school has come, park the car aside.

Joy parks the car aside and gets off to see Misti at the school gate.

Misti: Go back; otherwise, you will again pay a fine of 750 kroner.

Misti was imitating Shree and Maa, who frequently reminded Joy to follow the rules, as Joy had paid a good sum of money in fines. His stories of getting caught by traffic police are often a topic of enjoyment during social gatherings.

Actually, once Joy had parked his car in the parking place wherein free parking was allowed only for 15 minutes, as it was on the main road, you will find paper clocks in one corner of the main screen of the car. People set their time here when they use such parking, just for the traffic controller to know whether 15 minutes are over or not.

If you cross 15 minutes, then they charge you 750 Kroners as fine. This is done to maintain discipline in people. Once the traffic controller caught Joy manipulating the time in the clock, in between 15 minutes and sent a fine of 750 kroner.

Here the fine is not collected on the road, but the receipt is sent to your home after tracking address through the car number, and if you don't pay the fine on time then the fine increases and that is on the discretion of the statutory body to decide on the amount, as it is considered as case of gross misconduct.

Joy kisses Misti on her forehead and moves towards his car.

Joy starts his car and waves his hand as a sign of goodbye

Misti turns around and enters the school, and Joy drives to his office in Brande, which is 22 km from Herning. Joy works as a project manager for a leading multinational company that manufactures wind turbines.

Joy has been very successful on the professional front because of his work around ideas, just like wearing dirty socks by turning them around.

As Joy opens his mail to start his day, he receives an e-mail from his boss Ronald 'Come to my cabin. It's urgent.'

Joy takes his writing pad and starts walking towards Ronald's cabin. Ronald had the natural tendency to create hype. According to him, things are either extremely difficult or very easy, in between things that don't exist in his vocabulary and mind. If he could solve something, then it's very easy; otherwise, it's impossible for anybody to solve, and Joy utilised this very habit of Ronald to his favour by always giving his workaround solution at the end after Ronald had declared that as impossible.

Joy: God morgen Mr. Ronald (In Danish, Good morning is said like this).

Ronald: I wish that to be true, but that's not the case, I just received extremely bad news this morning and that's the reason I have called you on an urgent basis.

Joy: Tell me, sir, How I can contribute to making this morning good for you.

Ronald: Unfortunately, the customer of the Brazil project is asking for advancing the deliveries by 2 months, as a precondition for giving us the order whereas we have a float of only 15 days in the project. We cannot squeeze the deliveries by 2 months by any means and hence I was just preparing the draft mail to sales and marketing informing the same.

The reason I have called you is that now we are mostly not going to get the Brazil order, you need to pull some revenue from next financial year to this year to make up for the revenue deficit, as you are doing big ticket projects.

Joy: I have an idea, which I can propose if you permit it, sir.

Ronald: Let me hear what idea you have this time, as I have already worked out all permutations and combinations and pushed the minutes of meetings with purchase teams towards Joy.

Joy: Sir, is it not possible that we squeeze the schedule ourselves and accept the order ...making Ronald yearn for some more time for the solution ...

Ronald: How can you say that? Did you sleep last night? Is everything fine with your personal life, Joy? This kind of reply is not expected of you!!!

Joy: What I meant is that we reduce the delivery time subject to the condition that the client gives approval on all the documents within a week. As per the reputation of the consultant in the project, they would never approve documents before two weeks for review, so we will take an extension of the time later.

Ronald: What if they approve the documents within one week.?

Joy: Then as a backup we offer them the product for which we carry inventory so that we can match the delivery date.

Ronald (smiles): This is a good option. This day now seems to be not that bad.

Ronald: I just applied the technique of brainstorming and situational leadership to extract the best solution. This technique was taught to me during a management development programme at Harvard Business School.

Joy: How would I know sir; you never sent me for such courses. There must be very compelling reasons from your side, otherwise you always say that the first and foremost task of a manager is to take care of the growth of his subordinates. I can understand sir.

Ronald (smiles again): You are very clever; I get your point. Let me see what can be done.

Joy: I am always there to help you and contribute to your success; lifts from the seat and subsequently moves out.

> *Once again, Joy has proved his prudence and presence of mind before Ronald and has staked his claim for upcoming nominations for the management development programme at Harvard.*

Joy had a wonderful family, living in a place which is in the best country to live on the planet, had a job which he liked and had perfect balance between personal life and professional life.

> *Everything was going well in the life of Joy, like a smooth drive on a six-lane highway. It would have been an easy life and not a story worth telling, if it would have continued like this, however destiny had some other plans for Joy, some incomplete episodes were calling for completion and time for that is about to ripe soon.*

The Calling 'Calls'

While Joy was busy with his life, there were some developments taking place in a village of India, which changed the course of his life for the next few months. Why should we talk about it now? Well let's see!!!

It is almost 10 in the morning at Shantipur, a remote village in West Bengal (an eastern state of India), about 80 km from Kolkata, but Praful Mukherjee doesn't want to open his eyes, as he doesn't want to face this world for the time being. His exhausted body and mind are too fragile for the task he has been entrusted with. As destiny would have it, now it seems to be inevitable, and Praful Mukherjee would have to do this with an impeccable swiftness, which is so unlike him.

Praful Mukherjee is the uncle of our protagonist, Joy Mukherjee, who stays in Shantipur, their ancestral place and takes care of hereditary land and property.

Praful tries to look outside from the corner of his eyes out of hope that he will find something gratifying to bring him out of this melancholy. His eyes fell upon a pigeon relentlessly collecting the chaffs to build her home. The sun has almost covered half the distance of its paradigm, and people walking by are generously using their handkerchiefs to clear water out of their faces because of the lethal connivance of scorching heat and high humidity.

Praful closed his eyes to transcend into the past once again; just then, he was woken up by the voice coming from the window. It was of Shukla, a neighbour staying just on the opposite side of the road.

Shukla: Praful babu, today the results of matriculation have been declared and my son has stood 1ˢᵗ in the class.

Praful: Khub bhaalo (very nice), he has a bright future.

Shukla: Do you know how much percentage the second son of Rani scored? 45% huh...someday you will see him joining the weaving factories on the outskirts as a worker ...ha...ha.

Praful: Shukla, this world is like this because some people takes more pleasure in failures of others, than their own successes, and by the way it is more important to be a good person first rather than scoring good marks and Praful is much better person than that son of a wicked Santanu.

Shukla was taken aback by such criticism; however, as it goes with few people, they seldom change their stance and doggedly follow it to the gallows.

Shukla (sarcastically): You are completely inscrutable to me; maybe I am too young to understand your divine philosophy. By the way, who is this Praful? I hope you are not talking about yourself.

Praful was taken aback; the frequent shift between the past and the present has taken a toll on him, and he said something that he had heard years back. These words felt like the familiar smell of freshly bloomed hibiscus or somewhat like the smell of budding flowers on the mango tree or the smell of rice getting cooked in a coal oven. It resembled every smell that belonged to his childhood and got lost somewhere in between. Just then, he hears a jingle of the ice cream seller, and there is a sudden rush of collage of events. Praful conveniently closes his eyes again to soak himself in the nectar of the sweet memories.

Praful goes back to his childhood days.

Praful is running frantically with his friends. He is running as fast as a 5-year-old boy can so that he can ask for some money so that he and his friends can have some pickles. In those days, similar jingles were used by pickle sellers to call upon people to buy pickles. There were almost 20 varieties of pickles ranging from sweet to spicy. The diminishing sound of the jingle was an indication for Praful that he needed to get money and rush back to the pickle seller fast.

By the time they reached the house, they were all panting heavily due to their relentless sprint to the home. As soon as they regained their breath, they heard the synchronous blowing of the conch shells in tandem with the continuous wagging of the tongues by the ladies of the house. This is done on all auspicious occasions in Bengali culture. They were all dressed in traditional Bengali attire, adorned with ornaments and shakha-pola, which is considered a symbol of a married woman in Bengali culture.

He was accustomed to seeing his Grand Maa and Maa in such attire only during Durga pujo or Kaali pujo.

Lots of people gathered outside the house. They were murmuring something amongst them.

He seeped forward to see the reason for such a gathering.

Just then he heard his father climbing the stairs and people dispersing off. His father Protap Mukherjee had strong fascination with the sound of the boots used by the English people, he correlated the strong tap made by the boots to the manliness so much so that he got himself a special pair of sandals made of thick soles.

Now the intimation of his arrival precedes him, and he expects everyone to be prepared and be there, to properly receive him up to his satisfaction.

Protap Mukherjee enters the house with a thunder and waste no time to put his word 'Sukanto Chatterjee tricked me into getting his daughter married to my skilled son, but mind me, I also hail from Mukherjee clan and I would see to it that he pays a big price of resorting to such a demeanour, it is going to be a lifetime lesson for him.'

There is another village near Shantipur called Bishnupur, which is inhabited by the people with the surname Chatterjee, and Sukanto Chatterjee is the zamindar of that village. During one social function of a common friend, Sukanto and Protap, in a drunken state, got into a verbal altercation regarding which village has the better football team, and it got to a point where Protap Mukherjee stated that he was ready to do anything if a team of Bishnupur village can beat the team of Shantipur village and it was also agreed that Sukanto Chatterjee would wipe out his half-moustache if his team lose the match.

Protap Mukherjee led the entourage of his team with his son Projoy Mukherjee as the captain. Meanwhile, in a bid to save his half-moustache from collateral damage, Sukanto Chatterjee secretly called in a few skilled players from Kolkata city to play on their behalf.

No prize for guessing right that the Mukherjee team was made to run like a herd of cattle being chased by a tiger within a space of 45m x 90m. They were getting goals every now and then like a meowing cat.

Initially, there was a lot of aggression in their game, and there was frequent encouragement by Protap Mukherjee and other fellow villagers who had come to see the match, but after the 3rd goal from the Bishnupur team, they felt like a goat before the butcher.

Shantipur's team lost the match by 7-0, and Sukanto used this opportunity to get a daughter from his first wife, Anjali, married to the elder son of Protap Mukherjee, as a fulfilment of the condition for losing the match.

Protap Mukherjee agreed to relent but vowed to give a befitting reply at a suitable time in future.

As everybody moved aside, for Protap Mukherjee to move forward, Praful saw his boudi (sister-in-law) for the first time, a short girl with black eyes, still in her teenage years. She was looking like a doll in her bridal dress. Praful could see that she was crying. Soon she lifted her face to look around and their eyes met for the first time and they found somebody of their own in that very moment.

Those days there used to be a big difference between the age of the bride and the groom. In this case it was 12 years.

She always used to curse God for the sudden demise of her mother, as it had left her with nobody of her own to share her feelings and thoughts in a huge house filled with 25 relatives. Praful also used to feel like he had been trampled by all the elders of the family, where he was being used as a mere messenger to pass messages from one person to another. In moments of great despair, he used to wonder if the situation would have been a bit different at all, only if he had a sister.

Somehow, in that second, when Praful and the newly wedded bride exchanged glances, they felt like God was returning them something, for all the things taken away.

In the subsequent months, Protap Mukherjee tried his best to wreak havoc on his daughter-in-law, the new member of the family, but she didn't relent because of two reasons. First, she didn't have anywhere to go, and second, she had developed a very sweet and kind relationship with Praful, who would always make her smile, sometimes by bringing some pickles, sometimes mocking Protap Mukherjee and sometimes just singing Rabindra sangeet with her. In the evening, they would find a place in the corner wherein Praful would tell his boudi about all his experiences of the day, and at the end, boudi would tell him a story that he would love to hear. She was particularly very meticulous in framing interesting stories and singing songs.

Probably this quality God has instilled only in a girl that they start caring like a mother even before they become one.

The relation between Praful and his boudi became a symbiotic relationship of sea and a river where it is difficult to judge who completes whom.

Subsequently he and boudi became very good friends. Boudi used to help him with his studies, make him take bath, ensure he takes food on time and to give cue when Protap Mukherjee is at home.

In turn, Praful would secretly take boudi out when all the other members are taking afternoon naps, and they would spend the time flying kites by the side of a pond. Praful used to save money diligently from the pennies he used to receive from his elder brother and father for passing on information, and he used to get light refreshments for his boudi out of that meagre savings.

It so happened one day that Praful got to know that boudi was going to her maternal home.

Praful enquired to find that it had been decided by his father, Protap Mukherjee, that his boudi would go to her maternal home to spend some time with her family.

In the wrath of anger Praful went to his father and shouted, 'Why is boudi going to her maternal home?' Immediately he found his neck caught in one hand by his father, followed by continuous whipping of bamboo sticks on his butts.

Praful shouted as loud as he could, expecting against expectation that somehow his mother would muster the courage to face his father and would save him from this incessant bashing, just when he thought he was going to spend the rest of his life in this position getting his butt spanked, he saw his boudi running towards him and next very moment more than himself he was worried about his boudi.

Protap Mukherjee signed her to go back, but she stood quietly beside, holding Praful in her arm.

Protap Mukherjee. 'Nobody ever dares to speak over me here; this is my home.'

Boudi stood quietly.

Protap Mukherjee: 'I don't know what this child will do in future besides living on his father's money.'

Boudi was still quiet.

Protap Mukherjee got irritated by such a cold response. He shouted again at Praful 'See Santanu, he is excelling in all the fields be it sports or academics and see yourself. I think you should wash his feet and drink that water if that helps you.'

This time boudi replied 'It is more important to be a good person first rather than scoring good marks and my Praful is a much better person than that Santanu...' and walked away with Praful still in her arms.

Both of them were punished equally by Protap Mukherjee for such outrageous deception. Boudi was not sent to her paternal home and was allowed only one meal a day for a month and Praful was sent to boarding school to complete his remaining study.

However, whenever Praful visited home during vacation, they would sneak out of the home during the afternoon and talk their hearts out.

There was a smile on Praful's face, and he had a spurt of energy while he was reliving these moments in his mind. It seemed to be an event from yesterday.

Praful was wondering how destiny had moulded his boudi into a confident woman and took her from a village in India to Denmark. Now boudi is mother of an engineer son 'Joy' and beautiful daughter-in-law 'Shree.'

He tries to tilt his head to put it in the lap of his boudi and strikes his head to the wall.

Praful opens his eyes, there is a mirror beside his bed and he could see his wrinkle woven face with drooping brows and cheeks again. He felt a sense of loneliness as he couldn't see anybody from his dream around.

Nowadays the way of life has changed and has become more money oriented unlike before. Now a brother-in-law cannot have the same kind of openness with his boudi like he had enjoyed.

He still remembers the day, when Joy pleaded before him to convince his boudi to go with him to Denmark.

Nobody was able to convince her to go with her son to Denmark, until Praful agreed to take responsibility for the task entrusted to his boudi as a senior member of the family after the demise of his elder brother.

Somehow, Praful's worn shoulder is not willing to take that responsibility any further, not out of lethargy but out of age limitations and dependency on others.

Suddenly, the expression on his face changes from nostalgic to sheer determination.

Praful has decided now that this evening he would call boudi and would let her know that this year he would not be able to organise the ancestral Durga pujo because of his age and will ask for forgiveness from her.

Once upon a time this Durga pujo was one of the famous Durga pujo in the Northern part of the state, with people from high ranks in government office paying a visit to the ceremony.

The idol used to be brought from the famous Kumartully, with special decorations each year.

There was an arrangement of food for all the villagers for those four days of the pujo, and it was much talked about that because of the blessings of the deity Durga, the food used to be so delicious that the villagers used to eagerly wait for the Durga pujo to enjoy the food.

The villagers used to participate actively in the decoration of the pandal and it used to leave the outsider visiting the pandal with awe.

Many times, this ancestral pujo has even been covered by TV channels to show how the tradition of Durga pujo has been maintained in the Mukherjee family for many years now.

All the arrangements for the pujo were monitored by the members of the Mukherjee family, who used to come down to Shantipur from far-flung places during the pujo holiday.

But now over a period of time, very few family members are now coming to Shantipur for the Durga pujo as they prefer to use the holiday to relax in a tourist place rather than taking the effort to arrange for the Durga pujo.

Also, the choice of youngsters has changed a lot. They now wish to enjoy rock music and junk food during pujo in place of traditional music and humble offerings of khichuri to deity Durga.

Somewhere Praful Mukherjee was alienated by the flipping change in the taste of the worshippers. His age and his fond memories of the past Durga pujo has resulted in his denial to this wind of change.

He was not mentally prepared to accept this change from heart also he was not getting any support from his kith and kin, to lend the supporting hand in arranging the Durga pujo so he has decided lastly that he would withdraw from his promise to arrange the ancestral Durga pujo.

It's not always money that stops somebody from doing something; mostly, it's the lack of courage compounded by the absence of someone who makes you believe that you can make it happen.

The Calling 'Calls'

Just like a dusk sun gets reminded of its fall by the rising moon, Praful was getting reminded of the ascending emptiness by the ticking clock as it's soon going to be the time when boudi calls each day to know about his well-being.

As the hour hand touched the edge of six, Praful strengthened himself from inside as now the telephone could ring anytime.

Soon, the housemaid was at the doorstep to inform him that boudi had called up and asked for him.

Praful lifted himself from the cranky bed, reached out to slip in his slippers and slowly dragged himself to take the call.

Praful: Please take my pranam boudi. Hope everything is well at your end.

Boudi: I have taken your pranam and wish you a long and healthy life.

Praful: Don't give me this blessing boudi, times have changed a lot and I find it really difficult to adapt to the changing times and on top of this my rusted body is too old to repair.

Boudi: I cannot believe what you are saying. You were the first person in our village to wear suit pants, and if I remember correctly, you even had a photograph with a foreign lady sitting next to you.

I cannot believe that the world is changing faster than a dynamic person like you.

This time every day during the call, they used to talk of the old golden days and filled themselves with energy to accept the harsh reality that gone golden days are not going to come again. But today Praful was in no mood to get swayed by the talks as he had to convey bitter news to boudi.

Praful: I changed my clothes which were external, but people are now changing their tradition, their culture, their values, their basic foundation, things that makes them happy, things that makes them sad.

Boudi: What happened, Praful? You seem to be very upset.

There was a silence of a few seconds, which seemed like an eternity to both of them. Praful knew that it had to be now or never.

Praful: I cannot fulfil the promise of arranging the ancestral Durga pujo anymore boudi as all the family members are now interested to go to tourist locations during the pujo holidays and I alone cannot make the arrangements for the Durga pujo.

Before boudi could tell something Praful disconnected the call, as he knew that a slight request from boudi would have been enough to cajole him to reconsider his words.

Praful is disheartened and relaxed at the same time. He is disheartened for his boudi and relaxed as now he has conveyed what he was finding almost impossible to convey to boudi.

'The human mind unfolds itself in different manners, which sometimes makes our own reaction inscrutable to us.'

He went straight to his bed and closed his eyes to sleep; hoping that tomorrow will bring some good news for him, just not knowing what it will be.

Kolkata Kolkata!!!

It has been three days since Praful had disclosed his inability to organise the ancestral Durga pujo, however Maa had not disclosed this news to anybody. She had not shown any sign of sorrow, remorse, or a tinge of regret so it was business as usual.

Praful was eagerly waiting for the call from his boudi for the last three days. He couldn't muster the courage to call boudi out of shame. His last hope rested on the magnanimity of his boudi. Every passing day was like a solitary ordeal to an abyss of phenomenal pain. Every day, Praful would keep checking his mobile frequently, hoping that soon, the phone would ring and that boudi would be on the other side. Its late night in India so Praful goes to sleep after being assured that today as well the call from boudi will not come.

Meanwhile few hours later in Denmark, Shree was getting ready to sleep. Every day before going to sleep she would unfailingly spend ten min talking to Maa about the day and wish her good night. She entered the room to wish good night to Maa.

Maa: Come, Shree, sit beside me. She moved Misti aside to make some space for Shree.

Shree: See Maa, it is getting darker outside now at 11:00 pm. This is August, so within a month it would start getting darker outside at 6:00 pm.

Maa: Yes, winter is the time when I miss Bengal a lot. During winter, the entire ambience envelopes itself in some sort of magic. The fragrance of the freshly bloomed Palash, the melody of the baul song sung by the roaming monks, the blurry and foggy atmosphere, and everything concocts into something amazingly divine that cannot be described but can just be experienced.

Shree: On top of it, there are so many festivities during that time. So many melas, so many food preparations. The whole city gets dressed up like a bride. On top of it, we also have Durga pujo. Oh my God, how can I forget it? Do you remember that in the first Durga pujo after my marriage, Baba prepared rossogolas of the size of a football, just because I like rosogolla (sweetened milk powder balls)? It was such a fun.

There was a glow in her eyes and a smile on her face, a combination which makes every lady look beautiful.

Maa: How can I forget Durga pujo, who has given me a daughter-in-law like Shree? That day is still fresh in my mind. There was a Dhuruchi dance competition at our ancestral Durga pujo, and your father-in-law was the judge. You left everybody in the state of divine experience, the way you danced that day. Every move was impeccable and flawless, as if Goddess Durga was dancing to appease Mahadeva. That very moment, your father-in-law had decided to make you the wife of Joy and the mother of the flagbearer of our lineage.

There was a moment of silence, and then Maa started again.

I think you should try for the second child now, but...

Shree: But. What Maa?

Maa: I need to visit Goddess Kali to fulfil my vow so that you can conceive. I had pledged to visit Dakshineswar temple after your first delivery but somehow, I couldn't do that for one reason or the other and then I came here. You know Goddess Kali, if she is happy, she will give you anything you wish for and if she turns angry anything unfortunate can happen any time.

Shree: Maa, I don't believe in these things. I think now we should go to sleep.

Maa: I was thinking it would be good if we could go to India before the Durga pujo so that I can fulfil my vow and we can all enjoy our own ancestral Durga pujo. Misti is growing up and she needs to be connected with our culture.

But if I tell Joy, he will always find some excuse to avoid it. It's your duty as a wife to make him do the right thing.

Shree: Maa, let's talk about it some other day. Good night.

Ma: Good Night.

Shree was lost in her thoughts now. They have been trying to have a second child for some time now but without success.

Maa was also aware of this fact because before, she used to find used small black plastics disposed of properly in the dustbin, and she was well-read, she knew that it must be something related to birth control. It has stopped for some time now.

Also, she had taken up the topic of family heir with Joy and Shree many times and since last few months she could notice them smiling at each other and the smile is getting dimmer with each passing month because of obvious reasons.

Meanwhile, Joy was already asleep by the time Shree came to the bedroom. Shree quietly enters the blanket and puts her hand over Joy's chest.

Joy is too tired to make any movement. Shree remembered the days when Joy would wake up by mere touch of her and they would spend next one hour drooling over each other in different positions.

However now these adventures are reserved for weekends and that too lasts only for a few minutes. The sequence of events has become predictable and both go through it like a dedicated sportsman goes through workout diligently. Unfortunately, it requires dedication but not much passion.

Shree doesn't realise when she fell asleep thinking about all these things.

It was early morning, and Joy woke up out of thirst. He drank some water and turned to sleep again. His eyes fell on Shree. Her hair bunny has got loosened and her hairs are sprinkled over her face. The vermillion on her upper forehead was distorted and her left shoulder had leaned out of her dress to expose her birthmark. She was looking extremely beautiful.

Joy moved his hand over her face to gently mend her hairs and give her a lip kiss. Shree turned a bit in her sleep exposing herself furthermore.

Joy cannot sleep now. He pulled her close to him and started kissing her all over.

Very soon, they were both hands and gloved into each other.

While Joy was intimate with Shree, he noticed a different kind of smile on her face.

Joy stopped to enquire, 'Shree I can see you are smiling. Is there something you want to share?'

Shree: Hmm.

Joy: What?

Shree: Come closer...

Joy moves closer to her.

Shree: Come on, my lion, a bit more ...don't be so shy.

Joy was excited and perplexed at the same time. He pulled her on top of him, kissed her all over and whispered in her ears, 'Now, or you want more.'

Shree responded by moving closer to Joy and whispered, 'Nothing is going to happen by this until your mother pays a visit to Maa Kali temple as she had vowed.'

Joy was confused. He murmured: What?

Shree: Yes, Maa told me that yesterday, and you see, we have been trying for quite some time now, and I don't think you are such an underperformer, or are you? Shree was smiling again.

However, Joy was not in the mood to laugh, and Shree realised that.

She pulled him closer, rested his head on her chest and started scrolling her hand over his head to soothe him.

Shree: I have an idea. Why not go to Kolkata this Durga pujo? We would get to see all our relatives, Maa will fulfil her vow, Misti will get to see our culture and you have a chance of getting benefited along the way.

Joy: Me?

Shree kissed him and said: Well, we will see!!!!

Joy was sandwiched between two options, whether to visit a doctor to get himself treated or to visit Kolkata to fulfil the vow of Maa. Besides, it had been many years since Joy had visited Shantipur.

There is still some time left before the morning, so Joy thought of taking a short nap before the alarm rings up.

As he reached the office, he found a reminder from HR regarding the leave plan. It has been eight months of the leave calendar, and Joy has not taken most of his leave. They had planned to visit Spain during the summer, but they had to cancel it because of Misti's sudden illness. In Denmark, you need to give justification if you have not taken your allocated vacations.

The rest of the day went as usual for Joy and he didn't realise when it was 04:30 pm, while jumping from one meeting to another.

He thought of having some coffee and, meanwhile, took out his mobile to check his Facebook account.

He was scrolling down to check the updates from different friends. There were happy faces all around. One of his friends, Ramesh, had posted an amorous snap with his wife, whom he is getting divorced. Another friend posted his feelings about his father, expressing love, gratitude, and happiness; however, Joy is aware of the fact that in real life, this friend always had a difference of opinion with his father from childhood.

Joy thought, 'Facebook has become a book on your face which hides your real me from the world.'

It has been a hectic day, so Joy thought of returning home while picking up Misti midway.

As he returned home, he felt rejuvenated by the mesmerising smell of hotchpotch coming from the kitchen. It is an Indian dish made with Pulse, rice, and vegetables. It is normally cooked on a cloudy day and is an integral part of the Bengali fiesta.

He was reminded of his childhood when during Durga pujo the hotchpotch was being cooked in a huge vessel with two people using a spatula of the size of oars to stir it.

Though there were many occasions when hotchpotch was cooked at home, the taste during Durga pujo was something out of the world, even though it was prepared without special care and with special emotions.

Joy thought for a moment and realised that every incident since yesterday was somehow taking him back to Shantipur. Maybe this time he should visit Shantipur after a long time. He has been avoiding visits to Shantipur for several years now. Joy thought of taking a step back.

Just then, Misti pulled his hand: See, baba, how do I look?

Misti was dressed in a saree made from her mum's dress piece. She had also applied lipstick, bindi, and Kajal to her eyes. Joy was completely mesmerised by her look.

Misti would often dress up nicely to give surprise to Joy and Joy would bend on his knee to propose to her to dance like seen in Bollywood movies and at the end they would laugh at each other.

Joy was giving an unabated stare to Misti and so many thoughts were going on in his mind at the same time.

Misti: Come on, baba, on your knees.

Joy took a decorative flower from the vase and bent on his knees.

Misti gave Joy a blushing smile until he picked her up on his lap.

Joy looked around for Maa, and she was reading the book 'Mahabharata.'

Joy sat around her to give her a comforting hug.

Joy: How was your day, Maa?

Maa: It was good. Every day is similar.

Joy: Maa, I can see you have not spoken to Praful's uncle for a few days. Is everything OK?

Maa: Hmm. Why don't you talk to your uncle sometime.?

Joy: Yes, Maa, I need to talk to him. I need to transfer money for the Durga pujo celebrations. Maybe soon I will talk to him.

Maa: Yes, soon Durga Maa will visit our home again, there will be light, happy faces and long talks. Everyone gets dressed up in beautiful dresses, women apply aalta on their feet, that sound of drums in sync with the bell in devotion to maa Durga, tears were wailing through her eyes as she was speaking.

Joy: Maa.

Maa tries to speak while wiping her tears: yes, Joy.

Joy: Nothing.

He stands up to change his dress but suddenly sits back to complete what he has to say.

Joy: Maa, would you like to visit Kolkata during this Durga pujo?

Maa speaks, somehow concealing her delight, 'I would definitely like to, but talk to Shree and look at your professional commitments first.'

Joy: Maa I have looked at my professional commitments and have spoken to Shree as well. What do you have to say?

Maa could not conceal her happiness and burst into a smile. Sure, why not? Durga Durga

Joy stands up to go out. 'On one condition, and it's non-negotiable.'

Maa: What is it?

Joy: You will not take any vow to visit any temple without consulting me if it somehow impacts me in some way. In this case, in a big way... OK

Both understood what was being talked about.

Maa: Nodded her head for yes.

Joy: No. Say it. Say Yes.

Maa: Yes. I will inform Praful that we are coming to Shantipur this Durga pujo so that he can make the necessary arrangements.

Joy: As you feel right.

Shree was happy when she heard from kitchen about the discussion on going to Shantipur for Durga pujo.

She started to mumble a Bengali song out of Joy: 'Amaar Bela je jay....'

She got pinched in her buttocks, and as she turned around, Joy pulled her close and gave her a soft lip kiss.

She tried to look around for Misti. Joy let her know that Misti is watching cartoons now.

Joy pulled her closer and started kissing her again as Shree was moving her hand over his back. She slowly moved her hand down and whispered, 'Take your pinch back, Mr. Zamindar,' and they both started laughing.

There was a sudden silence as they heard Maa talking to Praful uncle curiously, they lent their ears there.

Maa: Praful how are you?

Maa: Yes, I am good as well. Listen, I have some good news for you. We are coming to Shantipur to celebrate Durga pujo this year.

Maa: No, don't worry, you need not do anything. Joy is like your son. He will surely lend a helping hand to the Durga pujo. Please tell all our relatives that I will be bringing nice gifts and perfumes for all, so they should all come to visit us during the Durga pujo.

Maa: Don't worry. I heard what you said last time. Maa Durga will make her own arrangements. Besides, I am not ready to believe that my Praful has become that old.

Shree started laughing. 'So, zamindar Babu, get ready to sweat for Durga pujo.'

Joy was relaxed. He thought that he would just help with coordination activities related to Durga pujo. How would he know that destiny had a different plan for him this time?

Meanwhile, Maa was praying to God, 'Maa, we are such a minuscule creature before your divinity. We don't have the capability to serve you. It's only you who has the generosity to give us a chance to feel your august presence between us for a few days in a year.'

Guide my son in the right direction and give him the capability to worship you and inspire others to do the same. Durga Durga!!!

It is said that there are supernatural powers in the prayers. It has powers to move the mountains and dry the sea. Maa has not asked anything even closer to that but let's see how it goes.

One month later

Joy woke up to an announcement: 'We will be landing in Kolkata shortly. You are not allowed to use the washroom now. Kindly ensure that your seat belts are fastened, your seat is in an upright position and your window is open.' Joy realised that he had couched into a seat like a baby while sleeping. He looked around to find Shree talking to Misti. Maa is looking abashedly through the window to get the first glimpse of the beloved city 'Kolkata.'

Suddenly, Maa yells in excitement, 'There, I can see Howrah bridge' Shree and Misti peek out to see that.

The plane was hovering over Howrah bridge. The first glimpse of the Howrah bridge from the top was breathtaking and magnanimous at the same time. Meanwhile Joy was making the futile attempt to identify his favourite sweet shop from the top.

Misti enquired, 'Would we go over this bridge?'

Joy gave an affirmative nod, and Misti started jumping on the seat in excitement.

Joy was filled with so many thoughts at the same time.

He was excited to see the changes and similarities in the city from the time he was out of here. He was excited to untie this jigsaw puzzle.

Soon, the flight landed in Kolkata, and they started preparing to disembark the flight.

Joy noticed that just like in Europe, as soon as the pilot switched off the engine, all the passengers stood up to queue up near the exit, even when airhostess is instructing them to wait, as if they were imprisoned in a jail and now they are getting released.

Praful had already informed them that their house helper Gopal was going to receive them at the airport.

So as soon as they came out of the airport Joy started looking out for Gopal but he couldn't be found. He tried to reach him on the phone but he was not picking the call.

As a last resort, Joy went to look for Gopal in departures, and he found him standing there with a placard.

Gopal has become old now. Joy could see a mix of black and white hairs on his head which was once completely black. His hairline has moved back, and his hair has become wavy which used to be slicked down with a heavy dose of coconut oil. There is a small belly in an otherwise lean body giving a feeling that he ate something which he could not digest.

Joy admonished Gopal and asked him why he was standing there when he should have been there upon arrival.

Gopal replied innocently, 'I thought I would find you here. How can I forget this place? This is the place where we left you last time with Mashima and Boudi, as he used to address Maa and Shree. I thought you would come out of this gate. I had decided to run away somewhere else as the house felt completely empty without you; however, I dropped that idea thinking of Praful da.'

Joy slipped a packet of cigarettes into his hand, and this was enough to make him happy. A pack of cigarettes is an awesome gift for somebody settled with a smoking beedi as it is cheap. When you have a packet of imported cigarettes, you are sure to be a celebrity in your circle (at least for a few days).

Gopal quickly placed the pack in his pocket and started putting the luggage into the car.

He was very quick to touch the feet of Maa and Shree as a show of reverence.

Misti frowned and looked at Shree. 'Maa, why he didn't touch my feet?'

Shree smilingly looked into her eyes. 'Because you need to have white hair or a moustache for somebody to touch your feet. Do you have any of these?'

Misti understood the teasing of her mum and started damped squealing.

Gopal was prepared for this. He slipped out a big biscuit from his bag. It was a rainbow biscuit with four colours made from different syrups. It is made locally in Shantipur and is very high in sweetness quotient.

Misti was more than happy to have it and opened it immediately and took a big bite.

Joy was expecting that Misti would soon complain about the sweetness of the biscuit, but she liked it.

Joy felt a sudden rush of happiness and thought that something must be there which preserves your originality from the eyes of the world and nurtures it like the soil hides the roots of the tree from the outer world and continuously nourishes it, intertwined, and separated at the same time.

They settled themselves in the car. To the utter dismay of Misti, she had to settle in the lap of her mother. In Denmark, she had the privilege of a separate child seat; however, in India, children up to a certain age mostly ply on the lap of their relatives. It's not unusual to find eight people conveniently accommodated in a small hatchback car.

Driver and Gopal were sitting in the front seat and Joy, Misti, Maa, and Shree were sitting in the rear seat.

Joy looked around to find the same old Kolkata which he had left ten years back. The same yellow-coloured taxi with a black patch at the centre. The buses were still those old steel-coloured structures howling around the city. They crossed their designed life a long time ago. It has been there for so long that people have accepted them as a part of life, and nobody expects anything better than this. The roads are still the same, and there is no chance of expanding them further because of the huge construction around them. It has developed a unique skill in commuters; they can take out their car or bike from very little space, and that too quite swiftly. There were hoardings of the politicians of the different parties decorated on both sides of the road. It is the easiest method to ensure that people remember you. It is a classic implementation of the illusion of truth effect where you hear/read lies so many times that you start believing it is true. All these placards portray a very kind picture of each of these politicians. There are words like representatives of the poor, growth mindset and equality used for each politician on these placards, but you don't see the effect of that on the ground. It seemed that the growth clock of the city got stuck somewhere.

Joy was perplexed to see such similarities in the city he left and the city he sees now. He was frequently looking to the side mirror to confirm that he is in the present and it is not a dream.

Maa was also taken over by nostalgia. In Kolkata, she had the home of one of her aunts. She used to visit here with her mother-in-law and Praful. As she was only 13 when she was married to Projoy Mukherjee, who was 32 then, she looked forward to visiting Kolkata, where she had small liberties like going out on a street walk and having puchkas and cutlets with Praful. Puchkas is a street delicacy made of a hollow, rounded enclosure of flour filled with spicy syrup and potato.

There was one time when they went a bit far to Dakshineswar temple. They weren't such ardent worshippers of Maa Kali and the purpose was not to pay a visit to Goddess Kali but to enjoy delicious kochuri and daal sold outside the temple. They returned after many hours and that ultimately led to severe admonishment of Maa by the elders of the family.

Misti, as usual, was full of questions. She observed so many sweet shops across the road and was very quick to enquire about that to her mum.

Misti: Maa, why are there so many sweet shops here? Is it what we will get for lunch?

Shree: No Misti, as you know sweet is a dessert, something which you eat after maincourse. There are many sweet shops because people like to eat sweets.

Misti: That is why my name is sweet. She enquired as the meaning of her name in Bengali is 'sweet.'

Shree: Yes, so that we can kiss you any time and enjoy your sweetness.

Misti blushed on hearing such compliments from her mum.

They stopped in between to have tea and some light snacks.

Soon the car moved through Salt Lake and Joy could now observe the transition of Kolkata from a heritage city to a modern city. The narrow roads have changed into four lane roads surrounded by high-rise corporate offices on both sides. The appearances of people moving in the roads have changed as they are working in corporate companies and not regular shops.

Misti pointed towards the McDonald's and Burger King shop as she was familiar with that.

Joy and Shree were looking at each other. Their impression of Kolkata has taken a back seat. The very nature of Bengali culture to absorb the best from everywhere has continued. Somehow, Kolkata has managed to preserve both his old and new self at the same time.

It was a 3 hour's drive from Howrah to Shantipur so gradually they all fell asleep, after such a long flight journey.

Gopal woke them up just before they were about to reach Shantipur.

It was noon by now, and they could feel the heat outside.

Joy told Gopal to stop by a sweet shop to buy some sweets.

It is a custom in Bengal to take some sweets while visiting a relative. Joy thought to himself, 'That might be the reason for having so many sweet shops in here.'

Meanwhile, Praful was eagerly waiting for them. He had bought a new dhoti and kurta to welcome them.

He had insisted the cook to prepare Hilsa fish for lunch as Joy used to love it.

Praful had become a widower two years back after losing his wife, Gita, to a heart attack. Praful lived in the ancestral house with his elder son, Shom, and his wife, Shanti. They were both amazed to see the energy level of their father as if a new life had been infused into him. Shom is an obedient son and takes care of all the family farms for the family. It is a concern for him that he puts effort into maintaining the ancestral properties and farms for the whole year, but at the end of the year, the profit from the produce is equally divided between the family.

Praful also had a daughter named Putul. She is married off to Animesh who is a doctor and is settled in Delhi. They arrived two days back to attend the Durga pujo after cancelling their trip to Kashmir on the repetitive request of Praful.

Praful went to see the mirror for the fifth time to see if his hair was properly slicked or not.

When he was young, his boudi poked him frequently if his hair was not properly slicked. Though he has become old now, those words have stayed with him.

Just then he hears the taxi stopping by. He rushes to the window and tries to check through the curtain. He could see his boudi trying to step out of the car. Her face now has more wrinkles, there are black patches around her eyes however she still had the most magnanimous smile which kind of covered everything.

Shom extended his hand so that Maa could hold it to come out of the car. Shom and Shanti touched her feet as soon as she got out of the car.

Maa suddenly looked out the window to find Praful looking at him. It was like the very first exchange of glances they had several years ago when she was welcomed into this home.

There were tears of happiness wailing through their eyes. Praful came out to touch her feet. Maa stopped him in between, 'No need for this; we both are in our second childhood, so we are absolved from all these things.'

Shanti was more than happy to meet Shree. During her marriage Shree went out of her way to help her feel comfortable. She briefed her about the customs and nature of all the important members of the family, which made it easy for her to adjust to the new world. Though at that time Joy and Shree came for just a few days it had created a bond between the two of them that continued to be nurtured by both through WhatsApp calls.

Misti was confused to see so many new faces around her. She was meeting them for the first time. She had seen her friends being dropped off at school by their Grandparents and often enquired whether she had a grandfather. She was told every time that she had a grandfather in India. She had an image of a grandfather in a shirt and pants, and now, when Praful, who was in traditional attire, was introduced to her as a grandfather, she was quite confused and didn't understand what to do.

Joy was feeling at home. Everything in the house and surroundings remained as he left ten years back. The school in the neighbourhood still had the same corroded gate. The road width was the same and as usual was filled with potholes. There was garbage accumulated beside the road. The pond in which Joy used to take bath was still there. Same light post, same houses everything was so same except Joy who grew horizontally and lost some hairs.

They have a big ancestral house in Shantipur, with its own pond for rearing fish and a big garden filled with coconut trees, mango trees and guava trees.

As the house was built 100 years ago, its construction was a bit different from the houses found today. The kitchen is in one corner of the house with its own façade as people used to cook previously by burning coal. There is no attached bathroom and toilet as it is altogether located in a separate cluster, constructed specifically for that. In those days, attending to nature's call was impious, so everyone had to take a bath every time they went to ease their stomach. The pain doesn't end there. You needed to fill up water from the well before going to the toilet as there was no water connection there.

So, if you feel a sudden urge to go to the toilet and have not planned a good time for such activities, then you are very unlikely to make it without a disaster.

Meanwhile everyone has gathered in the main hall as Maa assisted by Shree started handing out gifts to all the family members. It is a wonderful gesture to show your near and dear ones that you were in their mind when they started their journey to their home.

Swiss watch for Praful, Shom and Animesh considering their importance to adherence to time. Beauty products for all the ladies and Swiss knife for Gopal. One bag was full of chocolates of different kinds for people to taste and enjoy. Special attraction was liquor filled Danish chocolates.

Everyone was happy to receive greeting cards drawn by Misti for them.

Joy took this time to take the tour of the house. The voices from his childhood are getting replayed in his ears. The helpers unloading sacks of grains from the bullock carts, the grandmas giving instructions to the cooks. Suddenly Joy realised that all those people are gone forever. Any old house is full of stories of people getting born, married, giving birth to children, ageing, and dying.

Joy looked out of the window to see many new constructions around his ancestral house. Many old buildings are being replaced by new buildings. Joy thought to himself that this ancestral house might meet the same fate soon.

Joy could also see from his window the pond where he used to meet his friends every day. Those were wonderful and carefree days. Joy looked at his Tommy Hilfiger T-shirt and realised how different he used to dress at that time.

Old Friendships

Joy had a group of five close friends in Shantipur in his childhood named Sharad, Moloy, Robi, Pihu and him.

Sharad is a son of a schoolteacher. He was a bright student and had always stood first in his whole academic career. He was very good in debates and extempore speeches and had the proclivity towards journalism. He believed that by pursuing that profession he can usher in positive changes in the society.

Moloy is the son of a businessman engaged in the weaving and selling of cotton saree. Moloy was very creative with handcraft. He was very good at painting, making sculptures out of clay, and making decorative items from bamboo, which is amply available in Shantipur.

Robi is the son of a sweet shop owner. He had one skill that he loved to eat and used to amaze people with his capacity to eat. He had such a capacity to eat that people would often suspect that he had some hidden demon in his stomach who was eating on his behalf.

Pihu is the daughter of a dance teacher, and she was very good at singing. She had a good hold on Rabindra sangeet and classical songs. Shantipur is a small town and normally boys and girls don't mingle around but Pihu didn't like the gossiping nature of the girls, so she befriended boys who don't like talking about people.

Now Joy, the protagonist of this story, had very good convincing power. Right from his childhood, he had the skills to convince anybody of virtually anything. Once, Robi hideously applied shaving foam to his cheeks to emulate his father. When Joy got to know this, he convinced

Robi that as he had shaved prematurely, all his cheek hairs are now uprooted, and now, he would not have a beard in this life. That left Robi obsessed for a few days until Joy found a solution that Robi needed to make his friends happy. If his close friends declared that they were willingly donating some of their cheek hair to Robi, then he could have his cheek hair back.

That resulted in Robi stealing ten rupees from his father and giving a huge party to Sharad, Moloy, Pihu and Joy. Robi contested for the reason of including Pihu in the party as she doesn't have cheek hairs. Joy included her as a witness of God to confirm Robi had fulfilled all the requirements for getting his cheek hairs back.

All of them had different personalities, but there was one thing common in them, and that was their love for a daily chat. To make it clear to the readers, this chat is different from chatting on the internet.

Every day in the evening, they would assemble in the parchment near one pond close to school. They would have discussions on general topics like football, politics, poverty etc. Robi would bring some snacks from his shop for everyone. Sharad would initiate the discussion with his views, and then everyone would contribute to that. They would make big decisions like how the country should be run. How should Sachin have played in the last match? How should the peak hour rush in local trains be reduced? Etc. In the end, they vow that they will correct all this if they get a chance to do so. Finally, Pihu would sing one Rabindra sangeet, and everyone would subsequently join her.

Normally, friendship these days is built on a veneer of symbiotic requirements, however their friendship was untouched by such nuances as it didn't had any expectations. It just had a thin string of good time spent together to tie them together. It was as innocent as a song of a cuckoo on a hot summer afternoon. There is no audience, and there is no expectation, just a satiating life song flowing seamlessly to lure everyone and quench their thirst.

They were not just happy-go-lucky friends but somebody who would stand by you in your odd time. There was a time when Pihu decided to stop her education as the girls' high school was in another town, and Shantipur only had one higher school, which was co-education. Her parents were against her joining a co-education school. Sharad went to meet her parents to convince them. When it was not successful, the complete bunch went to her home with sweets, which Robi lifted from his family shop. They all committed to protecting her and giving regular updates on school activities to her parents.

They kept on insisting until her parents bulged and agreed to get her admitted to a co-educational school.

Like a cycle of nature where night comes after day, autumn comes after summer and sorrow comes after happiness, their togetherness was recessed by a hiatus, in this case it is so long that they all have forgotten those memories.

Even Joy had not talked about his friend circle to Misti.

It is surprising how a small incident in life can carry so much explosive that it can burn down such a flourishing friendship in minutes.

It happened on the last day of the higher secondary school. This day holds a special place in the heart of every student because on this day they get a farewell party from their juniors with special hospitality and respect which students always dream of and secondly this is the day besides Sarasvati pujo when they get to wear their own dress other than school uniform.

Joy Maa Durga

Saraswati pujo is the festival to worship the Goddess of Knowledge and wisdom called Saraswati. This day all the senior students of the school arrange all the activities starting from arranging the temporary tents to place Goddess Saraswati to preparing food for the students. They all dance to the tune of drumbeats and have a great time together.

Besides the religious aspect, this day is also known as Bengali valentine day as this is the day students see each other in beautiful traditional dress for the first time and they get hooked with each other.

In the last Saraswati pujo, Pihu was looking extremely beautiful in the red cotton saree. She was a good singer as well so soon she became the heartthrob for all the boys in the class. However, she had her own group to hang out with, consisting of Sharad, Robi, Joy and Moloy so she kept abeyance from other boys in the class. This made some of the boys in the class jealous of their group and Deep was one of them.

He tried many times to talk with Pihu that day, but he couldn't succeed. He vented out his anger on her friends by puncturing their cycles. Once he was about to get caught by Joy but somehow, he escaped by climbing the school boundary wall. Joy somehow sensed that it was Deep, as all the other students of his class were there except him.

That day during farewell, Deep tried to reach out to Pihu again but without any success and the time was running out of his hand. He wanted to convey his feelings to Pihu and was impatiently trying to find a suitable opportunity to do so, but somehow not getting successful in accomplishing that and that was leading to frustration from within.

Soon, the party was over, and all the final-year students started going back to their homes. Deep was closely watching the movements of Pihu and her group to find his moment to talk to Pihu.

Soon, his moment came when Pihu told his group to wait outside, and she went inside the school alone.

Deep thought that she might have gone inside to see her class for the last time. He followed her to the school. Soon he saw her getting inside the ladies toilet so he thought that he would wait outside for her to come out so that he could talk to her. He was eating his nails in tension and thinking at the same time what he was going to tell her.

Just then he turned his head to see that Joy was also walking towards the school from far away. He didn't know what he must do, as this was his last chance. His hand was wet in anxiety. Every step of Joy towards the school was making his chance to talk to Pihu bleak.

He decides to enter the ladies toilet to talk to Pihu. He enters the toilet and finds Pihu washing her hands.

Pihu was shocked to see Deep inside the ladies toilet with her alone. She started crying frantically for help; Deep in his attempt to persuade her to keep calm, moved closer to her which panicked her further. Deep was about to run out of the toilet. Just then, he got a strong blow on his head. Joy was holding him by his collar and he was getting incessant slaps on both sides of his cheek.

Deep somehow mustered the courage to push Joy back and run away.

Joy tried to console Pihu, who was sobbing inconsolably. It was a huge mental shock for her, and she was still trembling in fear. It took some time for Joy to assuage Pihu and then when they came out of the school it was embarrassing to find many students staring at them as if they have done something wrong.

Moloy came out of the crowd to ask Joy, 'Deep told everyone here that he had seen you entering the ladies' toilet when Pihu was inside. Is this true?'

Joy felt a dagger ripping his heart off into pieces in a moment. His face had become red with a sudden rush of blood. He felt a big lump in his throat. He was unable to breathe. He wanted to cry, but he couldn't. He stood there still like a grave, without any reaction. Pihu wiped her tears and tried to tell the truth, but Joy stopped her in the middle by waving his hand.

It looked filthy for Joy to give any justification to his own close friends. He moved out with Pihu without speaking to anybody. This was the last time they all met. Joy started putting more effort into his studies and gradually got admission to an engineering college in Shibpur. Sharad also pursued higher studies in journalism. Malay and Robi stopped studying further and started looking after their paternal business of sarees and sweets.

The worst affected was Pihu, whose parents subsequently got to hear about the incident from gossip and out of saving their face in a small town they got Pihu married to some man ten years older to her.

She was helpless now as her group of friends was not there to fight for her. She expected that Joy would at least meet her, but Joy clearly told his domestic servant to tell all his friends that he would not like to meet anybody.

Gradually when Joy's father Projoy Mukherjee got to know about the incident he called upon father of Pihu and warned him of the dire consequences if he ever sees Pihu near Joy.

Unfortunately, the entire world has misunderstood the friendship of Pihu and Joy, and it is Pihu who had paid the biggest price for this.

There is a set of baskets in people's minds, and anything they get, realize or receive, they put in either of these baskets. When there is involvement of a girl and a boy, they put them in either of the two boxes, either love or siblings.

The beautiful and most pious relationship of friendship is seldom understood and honoured by people when a boy and a girl are involved.

It is wrong, but it is like a jungle rule which everyone follows without using their mind.

Many years have passed since this incident and since Joy is back to Shantipur after a long time it would be worthwhile to know what his close friends are doing these days.

Each day of life is a surprise gift, and as happens with surprise gifts...sometimes you may not like it!!!

Sharad

Sitting in the corner office of a highest-selling newspaper publishing house in West Bengal, Sharad was perusing different articles that were recommended for publication in tomorrow's newspaper. He is the chief editor and hence, responsible for what gets published in the newspaper the next day. He was not surprised that most of the articles were pertaining to rapes, molestation, and robberies because this is how journalism has been redefined in recent times. This type of news creates more circulation for the newspaper.

All human actions are defined by two basic reflexes: to get pleasure or to avoid pain, and when given a choice, anyone would prefer to avoid pain rather than to get pleasure. All the newspapers use this basic principle of psychology to create more readership. They publish news that people will read to be aware of the situations that can harm them, but as collateral damage, there has been a steep degradation of trust in the society, community, and fellow countrymen.

Initially Sharad fought very hard against this norm by advocating publication of inspiring, motivating and positive news, however soon realised that he needed to be on the top to change the system and he would have to follow the system to reach the top.

He had aligned with the key political parties, corporate houses, and film stars to establish a very symbiotic relationship with them, which was mutually beneficial and coherent with the time.

This has resulted in a situation where the front page is filled with the mismanagement and shortcomings of the previous government and the appreciation for the new initiatives by the present government.

The inauguration of a hair salon by a film star gets more space than cracking of the civil services exam by the son of a rickshaw driver.

Sharad was not like that from the start of his career. He had the energy, thrill and daring of a rebellious journalist. He wanted to bring in positive change in the society with the help of his voice and pen. He had written many outrageous articles and had brought into open many issues related to the government policies when he started as a journalist in a news channel. He had instilled a fear in the mind of the corrupt officers until one incident mellowed him down.

He was covering the news about how different Durga pujo associations were literally using force to get more money from the corporate houses so as to make their pujo grander. It was a sort of competition to show more power by each Durga pujo association by making their Durga pujo magnanimous.

It would have been the biggest news of that year if it had been published. However, before this could happen, Nata Mallick, who was the general secretary of one of the big Durga pujo in Kolkata (Calcutta at that time), learned about this. He got him picked up from his home by goons and tortured him for four days and at last set him free after repeated pleading by him, and that too on one condition that he would drop his investigation on the Durga pujo funding topic and hereafter would not poke his nose into contentious issues.

Soon, Sharad became smarter; he started covering news which showed powerful persons in a good light and, as a result, started moving higher in rank. He already had the skills of a good journalist, and now, with his newly acquired smartness, he gradually and steadily moved up the rank and became the chief editor of the highest-selling newspaper in West Bengal.

It was late evening, and he was done with his editing task for the next day's newspaper. He reached out to his phone to check if there were any missed calls. As a habit, Sharad would always keep off his mobile while doing the final editing for the next day's newspaper.

He saw a voicemail from Praful kaku. When he called up to hear the voicemail, it was a familiar voice. 'Hi Sharad, this is Joy; sorry for calling so late, but I want to tell my side of the story. Please come and meet me this coming Sunday at our meeting point near the pond. I am counting on you to come.'

Sharad didn't call back later to talk to Joy, as he thought that it would make sense to talk to him face to face.

A few days later, one of his assistants, who was aware that Sharad hails from Shantipur, brings to his table an article published in a newspaper. There were many familiar names in the article and an opportunity to avenge his beating by Nata Mallik.

Sharad was now more than eager to visit Shantipur this coming weekend.

Robi

Robi was the healthiest member of their friend circle. He had a big belly protruding out of him like a tongue. He had four distinguishing features in his personality. Firstly, his thick arms and swollen cheeks used to give him an angry look whenever he was quiet; secondly, his small teeth and small legs portrayed the look of a small child. His legs looked even smaller when he used to wear pants because the beltline would often slip below the belly. All their classmates used to tease him by saying that he must often check by holding his carrot to confirm whether it was inside or outside the pants. Robi eventually got fed up, and then he started wearing a dhoti to ward off frequent pestering by the other students, but then they started saying Robi switched to dhoti because his carrot wanted fresh air. It was getting too much for him to endure until one day, he picked up a fight with a group of students over pestering him. Though he had thick arms, he wasn't good at physical fighting, so eventually, fists started flowing on him from all directions, and he thought that soon they would fling away his dhoti. But just then, Sharad, Moloy and Joy entered to rescue Robi. They pulled the students out of him and picked Robi up. Meanwhile, one student was still raging at Robi, so he tried to slap Robi from sideways, and it landed on the cheeks of Joy, and that was the only mistake they made that day.

Joy, Sharad and Moloy turned around and started beating the other group mercilessly. Robi also took this chance to polish his hands on those students who unreasonably pestered him for months.

Joy warned all of them to stay away from Robi and stop pestering him, or else they would be beaten again.

The next day, Robi brought a big packet full of sweets to the school for his new friends Sharad, Joy and Moloy to further cement his friendship with them. However, it was difficult to find a place to eat because if they opened the packet in the classroom, then all the students would come to take their share, and their portions would be reduced.

At the end, after much deliberation they decided to meet beside the pond near the school, in the evening to savour the delicious sweets.

In the evening, Robi met them near the pond, along with a packet of sweets and freshly fried snacks. Thus started the first of many meetings they had near the pond.

They talked about school, football, politics, types of sweets and many other topics but never made fun of Robi. They all enjoyed it a lot, and at last, Robi had someone to call a friend who accepted him the way he was.

Though being so mild, Robi was a monster when it came to his appetite. He would put even grown-ups to shame by his capacity to eat. His first achievement was winning the food challenge of Shantipur by eating three plates of chicken biryani. They gave him a small idol of a gluttonous man with a big belly and folded arms. His father, being a confectioner, was also very proud of this achievement of his son and had placed the idol in the front corner of his sweet shop.

Robi was often invited to attend social functions where he could showcase his gluttony. Soon his friend group also started joining him in such functions because it so happened a few times that Robi ate so much that he was unable to come back home by himself.

These days, he runs the sweet shop, which was previously owned by his father. There are seven little idols of the gluttonous man standing on the side display, which is proof that Robi has won seven food challenges. There was a vacant space in between the seven idols. The size of the sweet shop is the same as it was 12 years ago, but there has been a substantial increment in the earnings because of the rabid nasal sense of Robi. He would invariably taste the first lot of the sweets made from each batch himself and would get to know whether the sweets were made in the right way. He would resort to severe bantering of his staff if it was not found up to his taste. On the weekend, he would keep the special breakfast menu, and it was so delicious that people would stand in queues for hours to buy it.

He is married, and his wife and son look as plump as him. He had not made any new friends. Sometimes, he meets Pihu to talk about good old times.

Joy was aware that Robi liked good scents, as that would ward off the smell of sweets coming out of him Robi was particularly conscious of the smell of sweets coming out of him because of him helping out his father in the sweet shop.

So, he went to meet Robi with Misti, Shree, and a bottle of scent from Denmark. Robi was agitated initially since he thought that Joy had stopped talking to him because of differences in social status, but soon it dissolved when he got to know that Joy had brought a scent bottle for him from Denmark. He was also happy to see Misti and Shree.

Since he could not vent his anger, it had to come out before things could be normal again.

Joy was very much aware of this, so he told Robi that he would like to clarify things with him at their meeting place near the pond this coming Sunday.

Robi nodded his head in affirmation while handing over a pocket full of sweets to Shree.

There wasn't any lengthy talk, but it was a good beginning after years of gap.

Moloy

oloy is the son of a businessman. His father was a wholesaler
of cotton sarees. They had many weavers working for them.
His father was very miser and would pay the least possible money to
the workers for weaving sarees for him. His father would often visit
Kolkata to sell the sarees to the retail shop owners at premium prices.
Shantipur is known for its sarees with uniform textures and is known by
different names based on its border, such as Ganga Jamuna, Nilambari,
etc. His father would often send Moloy to supervise the weavers and to
ensure that they completed their tasks on time; however, Moloy would
invariably end up talking to them about weaving and other forms of
art. Moloy made the weavers feel appreciated by asking questions and
being inquisitive. He was very fond of clay painting. He painted the
boundaries of this house, portraying different daily chores done by
women, such as washing clothes, cooking, cleaning, etc.

Moloy would get frequent bantering from his father for indulging
in painting, crafting, and other creative works, which, according to his
father, was a complete waste of time. His father was worried about
his future, so he would often insist that he learn the nuances of the
trade, but he would hide in some corner of his house and would spend
hours painting or creating some sculpture or creating different shapes
out of newspaper cuttings. It had a healing effect on Moloy, and it was
the time when he would transcend from this world into his imaginary
place, which is full of art and creativity.

Joy and Moloy became friends in biology class because of Joy's
exceptional sketching talent. It so happened that the teacher had given

them a task to draw the digestive system and show different parts of it. Joy was so exceptionally poor in drawing that when the teacher looked at his sketch, he asked Joy, 'Joy, your large intestine and small intestine look almost similar, and they look more like a long stretch of poop' Joy replied, 'Actually, I had a lot of biryani yesterday.' What followed later was a series of smacking by scale on the open palm.

At last, the teacher showed him the sketch by Moloy and told him to talk to Moloy and learn how to draw the digestive system.

Joy and Moloy spoke to each other for the first time, and they soon became very good friends. Joy introduced Moloy to Sharad, and they became an awesome threesome.

During the final examination, Joy and Moloy exchanged paper, and Moloy sketched Joy's digestive system as well.

When the teacher was checking their paper, he understood something is fishy, so he took a jibe at Joy. 'Your digestive system and Moloy's digestive system is almost same, are you twins' to which Joy replied, 'Actually we were together yesterday, and we both had fish cutlets, you can see fish bones in both of the drawings if you look closely' and the complete class broke into laughter.

These days, Moloy is running the saree business of his father as well as teaching paintings and sculpture making to the poor people so that they can earn a living out of making and selling clay dolls and simple handicrafts. Gradually, there were many new businessmen in the town, manufacturing the sarees using modern machines, whereas Moloy had manual looms used in the time of his dad, which he didn't bother to replace as he didn't have any interest in the business.

Moloy

He had established a perfect balance between the expectations of his father and his own personal ambitions.

He is married and has a daughter of 10 years named Trisha. They live a normal life which doesn't have the grandeur of a rich man and the misery of the poor, and importantly, Moloy has found the balance between expectations of his father and his own desire.

Moloy heard of Joy's arrival from his neighbors. He was in two mind, whether he should visit Joy or he should wait for Joy to make the first move. Moloy had lately realized his mistake of not taking stock of the situation on the last day in the school and asking Joy the stupid question "whether he went inside the ladies toilet?" before so many friends.

It has been years and with maturity his perspective of life has also changed, so Moloy decided to go and visit Joy at his home. He saw Misti skipping on the veranda and Praful kaku reading the newspaper. He thought that maybe Joy was not in the house and that this was not the right time to come, so he turned around to return, just to face Joy.

Moloy was taken aback, but before he could collect himself, Joy gave him a tight hug. That was sufficient for Moloy to forget everything and reciprocate to Joy. He has also matured to understand the fact that some answers can wait, but some moments, if not enjoyed, never come back.

Shree joined them with some refreshments, and they talked at length about their life. Shree was overjoyed to know that Moloy owns a saree weaving yarn and promised to visit the place with Maa and Misti.

Shree is a trained dancer so she has the natural liking of the people engaged in arts and crafts.

Joy informed Moloy about the upcoming get-together near the pond.

Moloy enquired, 'Have you met Pihu?'

Joy informed 'No, I am planning to, and I would need your help here.'

Moloy nodded and responded: 'I know you do.'

Pihu

life changed drastically for Pihu after the incident on the last day of the school. There was frequent coercion from close relatives to get her married, and ultimately, her parents got her married off to a person ten years older than her when the marriage proposal came from a government employee. In villages, government jobs still hold a great esteemed value and are the most secure proposal for the girl's future. Many people don't see the utility of educating their girls, but they forget one simple thing: how an uneducated mother will educate their grandchild. You learn so many skills in your education that come in very handy in cruising through life, and life doesn't always mean only an office job and salary but includes all other aspects as well, like social circle, empathy, mannerisms, respect, etc.

Subsequently, Pihu got pregnant and gave birth to a daughter, Ruchi; soon, his husband, Shambhu, started pressuring her for a second child as he wanted an heir to the family. But their economic condition was not good, so Pihu insisted on waiting for a few years so that they could pamper Ruchi till she is atleast three years old. Her husband couldn't accept this rejection and threatened to divorce Pihu. He would also beat Ruchi often to vent his frustration. Ultimately, Pihu got fed up with daily bullying and divorced Shambhu. She now lives with her mother and Ruchi in her maternal home. She got the job as a music teacher based on Praful kaku's recommendation. The income is somewhat sufficient to spend 20 days of a month, so Pihu also takes music classes besides her job to make ends meet.

Though they have financial constraints, they are living a happy life. They would still buy an ice cream, but it would be shared in three parts between Pihu, Ruchi and her grandmother. They would still go to the garden, but they would walk for 3 km rather than taking a rickshaw. They are a close-knit family that takes on every day, as it comes.

Pihu had just returned from her school and was getting ready to have lunch. Just then, there was a knock on the door.

Pihu reaches out to open the door and finds Moloy and Joy outside. She makes way for them to enter.

Joy entered the room and touched the feet of Pihu's mother.

Pihu volunteers to start the discussion with Joy. 'So, Joy, you must be very happy with Shree and your daughter in Denmark.'

Joy didn't know what to say, so he asked back to Pihu. How are you?

Pihu replied, 'I am doing good.'

Joy noticed the change in her, as now she has learned how to lie flawlessly.

Joy diverted his attention to Ruchi' Whom do you like more, your father or your mother?

Ruchi replied, 'I only have a mother; my father has married another girl, and she is not my mother. I love my mother a lot.'

Joy felt a lump in his throat. He didn't know what to say. Moloy had tried to stop him the moment he asked this question.

There was a complete silence in the house. Ultimately, Pihu's mother intervened. 'Why don't you take your lunch here? Pihu, please insist on them.'

Joy and Moloy said in Synchronisation, 'No, It's O. K. We are just about to leave.'

But Ruchi insisted. 'Come on Uncle I like to eat food with many people and it's only Moloy kaku who visits us.'

Pihu served them food and insisted that she and her mother would eat later.

It was only rice and dal without any accompaniment, but Ruchi was eating it with a lot of excitement and happiness because she was happy to have them for lunch.

They finished their lunch and asked for permission to leave.

After they were gone, Pihu closed the door and looked at her Maa.

It was an indication that today, they would have to skip lunch.

Maa suggested eating some Muri, which is a form of dehydrated rice.

Pihu brought some Muri to eat, but there was a knock on the door again.

It was Joy with a packet.

Joy handed over the packet to Pihu and said.' I am extremely sorry Pihu; I should have handled my anger better and should have come out to help you. I don't know how I will take out the burden of that regret. But we all are meeting again at our meeting point coming Sunday at 5 pm. I would request you to also come.

Meanwhile, don't eat only Muri. It tastes better with Vegetable cutlets, and for Ruchi, there is a packet of popcorn.

Joy returned home after a hectic and tiresome day, both physically and mentally. He tells Shree to serve the dinner early as he would like to take some sleep. Shree arranges dinner for Joy early and sends him to get a good night's sleep.

When Shree comes to the room after completing the household chores, she noticed that Joy was crying before he slept. She moves her hand over Joy's hair, and Joy pulls her close to him as soon as he realises her presence.

Shree asks Joy about what is bothering him, and Joy narrates the complete sequence of events from the morning.

Shree replies, 'You should be happy that you have such good friends, nobody can change the past, so let's put effort into changing the future.' Shree continued, 'Can I also join you on Sunday to meet your friends? I would also like to meet such wonderful people.'

Joy gave an affirmative nod.

Durga Pujo

While Joy was meeting all his old friends and acquaintances, since it had been some days since he was in Shantipur, so he thought of taking up the topic of the Durga pujo arrangement with his uncle Praful. Joy used to address him as kaku.

Joy: Kaku, how do we plan to arrange the Durga pujo this time? Let me know if you need any help.

Praful: Joy, would you please bring my support staff lying behind the door?

Joy picks up the support staff and hands it over to Praful.

Praful stands up with the help of the support staff and walks out of the door while waving for Joy to follow him.

They crossed the kitchen, which was on one side of the house, to face a 50m x 50m open space vegetated with wild grass.

Praful uses his staff to point to the ground. 'This is the place where we used to have our ancestral Durga pujo.' It was such a grandeur for those four days. The whole village used to assemble here for those days. There used to be many cultural programmes and competitions between intellectuals through the rhythmic use of words, singing, drawing, etc.

Those days Bengal used to be the cultural capital of India. All the famous movie stars, politicians, singers used to come to the villages to celebrate Durga pujo as it gave them the taste of the cultural heritage.

Joy remembered from his childhood how once, during Durga pujo, they went to see the programme of famous singer Kumar Sanu. There was a huge crowd, and the singer also enjoyed the huge applause he received at the end of each song.

Praful rested himself on the pavement. 'How do you think your father was?'

Joy took a deep breath. 'Strict...hmm, very strict.'

Praful took a jibe on Joy. Who can understand it better than you? But did you know he had a kind heart as well? There was one such time when all the village's produce was destroyed because of the heavy rain. Your father willingly opened the doors of our inventory to help the villagers survive. Do you know what your father said when I asked him, 'How will we manage?'

Joy enquired, 'What?'

Praful replied, 'Your father replied that Maa Durga will take care of everything.'

Joy took this opportunity, 'Yes that's what I was asking how we are planning for the Durga pujo this year?'

Praful lifted himself again and signed Joy to follow him.

He reached below a big mango tree on a corner of the ground.

Praful said, 'Here the cook used to place the big utensils to cook food during Durga pujo. Misti would be shocked to see the size of the utensils. Do you know what you said to me when you saw those utensils for the first time? Do you remember that?'

Joy: No, kaka

Praful: You started crying, and when I asked why you were crying, you replied, 'Will these people cook me as well? Ha...ha... ha...,' Praful started laughing loudly.

They saw Shree and Shanti coming with tea and some chairs.

They all sat below the Shade of the mango tree.

Joy tried to make fun of his Kaka 'Kaka the meal prepared for the deity Durga is always very delicious. Maybe the faeces of crows has something to do with this.'

Praful also smiled back with the response, 'I have not tasted the faeces of the crow, so you may be right here' And everyone couldn't restrain themselves from the sudden gust of laughter.'

Praful looked at Shanti and Shree and asked with his penchant smile, 'Do you know why we celebrate Durga pujo?'

Shanti was first to respond, 'We celebrate Durga pujo as this is the time when Goddess Durga comes to visit our world with her children Ganesha, Kartikeya, Saraswati and Laxmi. In these four days, we welcome them, we worship them, we offer them good food, and at last, we bid them farewell for the journey back to her husband, Lord Shiva's house.'

Praful nodded his head. 'Yes, I grant you passing marks but not good marks. Shree, would you like to try?'

Shree gave Praful a thoughtful glance and started speaking slowly.' I think we celebrate Durga pujo to celebrate life. These are the days when we move out of our daily schedules to spend time with our near and dear ones. We discuss our joy, our sorrows, our moments of triumph, our moments of disappointments. We completely empty our hearts in front of Maa Durga and seek strength from her to face this world again. We seek strength to maintain our morality and dignity in all kinds of adverse conditions.

Sorry kaku, I am aware of the mythological episode of Mahishasura, about how Mahishasura had weakness towards Maa Durga, and she was left to herself for her protection as he had obtained a blessing from Lord Shiva that no man can kill him. But I still think the main reason we celebrate Durga pujo is to stop for a moment, acknowledge and celebrate different aspects of life.

Praful was very happy to hear this; however, he still turned towards Joy to expect any response from him.

Joy replied, 'Common Kaka, we already have a winner here. Whatever I say, it would go in vain. But What I am concerned about is this year's Durga pujo, and somehow, you have been avoiding this question for some time now. What have we planned for that?'

Praful was quick to respond this time. 'Yes, what have YOU planned for the Durga pujo this time?'

Joy was mesmerised. 'Is it me? He was blabbering in confusion.'

Praful took this opportunity to speak again. Yes, of course, you are our heir, and you will take our tradition forward. I have planned for Durga pujo for years now, and this time, I want you to make all the arrangements. I will sit in the corner and give you my blessings. You know, I have seen your father personally looking into Durga pujo' s arrangements. After he expired, it was your mother who took over the charge, and then it was me. Now, it's time for the next generation to take over the mantle. Next year, I know you will not be here; I don't know whether I will be alive or not or your Maa will be alive or not. So, I leave it to you to arrange this year's Durga pujo.

Joy interrupted. 'Don't do this, Kaka; I will not be as good as you.'

Praful was swift, 'You are right, you will be better!!!'

Joy realised that Shree and Shanti were also following the conversation, and his self-respect was at stake now.

There was silence for a few seconds until Joy repeated, 'I grant your wish, let it be me.'

That evening, Joy went to Bisnupur to drop Maa off as she wanted to stay in her maternal home for a few days.

Maa had not visited her maternal home for several years now, so she thought of staying there and spending a few days with the children of her cousin brother Byomkesh.

Byomkesh had two sons, Rakesh, and Rajesh, who were approximately the same age as Joy.

Joy received a warm welcome at his maternal uncle's home. They got hold of Joy after a long time, so Joy was getting special hospitality from every member of the house. This was not going well with Rajesh and Rakesh who had never seen another man getting so much importance from the ladies of the house.

Byomkesh enquired, 'So Joy, what do you do in Denmark to make a living?'

Joy replied, 'I am a project manager. I execute wind turbine projects wherein we produce electricity from wind energy. The value of a normal project is approximately ten Crores.'

Byomkesh had not asked about the value of the project here, but Joy told this just to create a big impression in the minds of the people around and to tease Rajesh and Rakesh.

There had been many instances in their childhood wherein Rakesh and Rajesh had played pranks on Joy, and since Joy was alone, he was the one who was later persuaded by all to make up with them.

Rakesh opined. 'So, you must be really busy handling such big projects?'

Joy replied, 'Not like you. You have never found time to visit Shantipur in the last two years.'

Maa understood the situation and intervened, but it did more damage than help.

Maa. Rakesh and Rajesh, this year Joy is going to arrange the Durga pujo, and you need to help him here.

Rakesh quickly said, 'Yes why not, it would be our pleasure to help Joy, but Joy do you need any help from us, as you might have executed a much bigger project than this.'

Rajesh further nailed it: 'Sure, we would help you. We still talk about the football match which your grandfather lost to our grandfather; this is a win-win situation for both of us. No casualty.'

Joy was grinning with anger; his face had become red. He was trying to suppress his anger somehow.

Rajesh further opined. 'Don't worry, Rajesh, our Durga pujo was awarded the best Durga pujo in southern Bengal, so we will help you to be second this time and start laughing.'

Don't be mistaken. They were not enemies, but their relationship was such that it was full of such episodes.

Everyone has seen such exchanges so many times between them that they have got used to it, but they forgot one small change that is now they all have grown up, married and have kids.

Joy gave a thought for a moment and then said, 'Do we have any prize for the runner-up?'

Rakesh laughed it off. 'Yes, it was a garland of flowers.'

Joy smiled back. 'So this is what you both are going to get this time. Because the first prize belongs to Shantipur this year, it will be the best Durga pujo in the whole of Bengal.'

Subsequently, Joy came back after dropping Maa in Bishnupur, and everything was back to normal until two days later.

It was evening and Joy was figuring out how he will plan for the Durga pujo sitting on a couch in his room and Praful entered his room with a piece of paper in his hand. He has a meeting with his friends this Sunday, so he had planned to ask for their help as well in this venture.

Just then, he heard the increasing volume of support staff stomping and hinting at Praful kaku's approaching.

Praful enquired, 'How was your visit to Bisnupur?'

Joy replied without looking back at his kaku. 'It was good, why?'

Praful replied. 'Because there is one article in the local newspaper that the zamindar of Shantipur is back this time for Durga pujo, and he has pledged that this year their Durga pujo will be the best Durga Pujo in Bengal.' He extends the newspaper to Joy.

Joy takes the newspaper in his hand and frantically starts reading the article. One journalist interviewed Rakesh, the elder son of Byomkesh, his maternal uncle, regarding their preparation for Durga pujo this year. Since last year, they have been judged to be the best Durga pujo in the southern region of Bengal. Rakesh responded by saying that this year they are making extra preparations as he has received a challenge from the zamindar of Shantipur, Joy Mukherjee, that his pujo will be the best Durga pujo not only in the Northern region but in the whole West Bengal state.

Joy thought to himself that this time Rakesh and Rajesh had taken this too far, and now he is left with no choice as it is now known publicly.

Praful said.' Do you remember you had a friend, Sharad? He is now editor in a big newspaper. l will get his number and l will call him tomorrow. We will figure out how to deal with this.

Praful left the room with Joy, still figuring out what to do.

Joy moved around restlessly in his bed as there were many thoughts going on in his mind. He was thinking how one event led to another, and he landed up in the present situation.

Just then, he felt a soft hand running over his head. He looked over to find that it was Shree.

Shree took his head in her lap and started moving her hands gently over his head.

Shree asked softly, 'What is bothering my teddy?'

Joy was silent.

Shree further asked. What?

Joy replied 'Nothing, l was just thinking of the present situation. l have not organised Durga pujo ever in my life and now for the first time l will have to organise the best Durga Pujo in Bengal. l don't know how l am going to do that.'

Shree whispered into the ears of Joy. 'When was the last time you tried to do something different with your whole heart and you failed?'

Joy smiled back. 'Many times, l was well below target, as confirmed by your highness.'

Shree pulled his bundle of hair while caressing. 'I am not talking about that. I have seen you achieve so many things in your life when you put in your best efforts. What I am telling you is not to resist this situation but rather embrace it, accept it, and invest yourself completely into making this event successful.'

It is immaterial whether or not it would be the best Durga pujo. What is important is whether it brings back hope in the lives of the people, a reason to smile, or an excuse to celebrate life.

Shree continued. 'I am completely sure that this event is going to be a great success. Now, for the time being, you keep the thought of Durga pujo aside for today. I am sure things will turn for the better starting tomorrow.'

Just then, a neighbouring house played conch as a ritual to mark the end of the evening and the start of the night.

They both looked at each other and smiled back as if it was a sign that things were going to be fine.

Next morning when Joy came down for the morning breakfast, he saw a mob waiting outside his home and his Kaka Praful discussing something with them.

Joy went out to see what the matter was.

The moment they saw Joy, they all started shouting, 'Our Joy is Joy Mukherjee!!'

Joy was unable to understand what was going on.

The amplitude was going higher and higher as he was coming closer to them.

Joy calmed them down by raising his hand and pointed them to settle down.

He looked at his Praful kaka, expecting some explanation on this.

Kaka explained. 'They are the villagers, and they have read the article about you in the local newspaper. They are here to show their support to you.'

One person stood up to speak.' It has been many years since that unfortunate football match, and we would like to avenge it this time. We are fed up with the frequent taunts from the people of Bishnupur village. Once, I went to Bishnupur village to find an alliance for my son, but it ended in a quarrel when a discussion about that football match came up.

You are our leader, and we are with you. We will surely make this Durga pujo the best Durga Pujo in Bengal.

All the eyes were on Joy, and they were expecting Joy to say something.

Joy raised his right hand and exclaimed, 'Yes, we will,' and there were deafening cheers in the crowd.

Reunion

Today is Sunday and this week has been really eventful for Joy, so many things happened in such a close timeframe that it was really difficult for Joy to put things in their perspective. However, he was really hoping that his friends would turn up today as planned to meet after a long time.

Joy went around just to remind Robi, Moloy, and Pihu about the meeting today, taking the excuse that he had just happened to come this way for some other important work.

While he had got everything he aspired for in Denmark, he always missed the good time he had spent with his friends. Initially, he was angry that his friends didn't understand him, but gradually, maturity taught him that he had also not put in enough effort to explain the situation about the incident on the last day of the school to his friends.

Shree could observe a different type of expression on Joy's face, which had shades of anxiety and joy concocted together.

Joy had already told Shree about his friends, the dispute episode and how their lives had changed after that.

It was around 4 pm, so Joy hinted to Shree to get ready since she wanted to join as well.

However, Shree responded, 'I will join a little late; you go and meet your friends first.' Since you are meeting your friends after a long time, it is better you meet your friends like yourself.

Joy's tension quadrupled after listening to this, but he understood that Shree had a point, so he got ready and set off in Praful kaku's cycle for the pond.

He thought of picking up Moloy enroute, but it turned out to be troublesome for him because Moloy assumed that like old times Joy would carry him in cycle and took the back seat.

When they reached the pond, Joy almost resembled a salivating dog, with their tongue protruding like a curtain caught in the wind.

Sharad was already there, so he came forward with bottled water. 'Drink some water; you need to talk a lot today.'

Joy was happy to see Sharad and he was reminded once again that Sharad used to reach before time every time they used to meet at the pond.

They settled themselves at their familiar corner of the pond, which has changed very little over the years.

Moloy started the discussion 'Hopefully Robi will remember to bring some samosa and Jilipi (it local version of Jalebi) with him today, they were awesome.'

Robi replied from behind with a laugh, 'Sorry, Jilipi will be ready in the late evening, but I have brought rasgullas.'

Since there was no formality in between them they started to indulge in enjoying the delicacy without waiting for Pihu.

After some time, they realised that Pihu had not come yet.

Moloy mentioned, 'Pihu has gone through a lot, so maybe she doesn't want to get scared anymore. I think we all should respect that if she doesn't come.'

Joy was silent, but he nodded in affirmation.

Sharad and Robi were looking at each other, thinking what to say.

Just then, Shree arrives with Pihu. Shree hinted that she and Pihu had a talk, and now she is aware of his side of the story.

Actually, Shree heard from Joy about his meeting with Pihu, and she quickly understood that she needed to talk to Pihu to convince her to forgive Joy and move forward.

Shree had spent many years with Joy, and she knew that Joy lacked the sensitivity to talk with women.

So, after Joy went to pick Moloy up from his home, Shree went to meet Pihu.

Robi handed over samosas to Shree and Pihu, and they all went to their usual meeting place and took their seats.

There was silence again as everyone was waiting for somebody else to start the conversation.

Shree started, 'Robi, you have made such delicious samosas that nobody is talking!!!!!'

Joy quickly responded, 'It has been years since we all sat like this. Once, this used to be our daily routine, irrespective of how occupied we all were. In the evening, we all used to leave everything and spare this time for ourselves, to talk our hearts out, to be ourselves. Time flies by, and now we all are parents ourselves. Sometimes, friendship is like that brick that cannot be compressed by any contingent situation, but an unfortunate single blow can make it break into two.'

For me, that blow was the last day of the school, when I was questioned in front of the whole class by my own friends. People whom I had trusted with my life, pushed the dagger in my heart. I was broken into pieces. I lost faith in people. Most of the people in my house were older to me and you were the only ones whom I could call my friends.

Joy is taken back to that day, and his anger is finally released as tears.

Joy continued, 'But years later when I saw people with many more differences forgiving each other and having a good time together, I realised that maybe I had stretched it too much. Maybe I should just forget that incident.'

It gives me immense pain to see how Pihu's life has turned out. She wanted to study further and carve a life for herself. I am also to be blamed for that.

Joy turned towards Pihu 'Please forgive me if you can. Trust me, I will do anything possible now to get you a better life.'

Joy was much relieved now. He has released the anger he had been carrying for years. He had been blaming his stars for not getting good friends, even after deserving one.

Moloy, Sharad and Robi were looking at each other, as they didn't think that this could also be a scenario. They were all stumbled by Joy's rendition of the situation.

Moloy chipped in 'Its Ok Joy. We also made a mistake that day. We should not have asked you at that time and later also when we saw that you are not comfortable, we should have rather supported you and Pihu.'

Robi asked Joy, 'Why are you suddenly saying sorry?'

Joy didn't think of any response to this, but he somehow mustered the courage and said,' Because I think I realised that we have wasted a lot of time which could have been used to enjoy with each other, so I thought of taking the first step.

Sharad took his cigarette and looked at Joy. 'So you took the challenge to arrange the best Durga pujo.'

There was silence.

Sharad said, 'You forgot that I am an editor, so no news like this would be hidden from me.'

Joy said, 'This was not the reason for calling you all.'

Sharad said without any expression, 'I have known you since childhood, so don't try to trick me.'

Moloy said "Are we still going to continue rest of our life just like this?

Robi was filled with guilt when he heard the Joy's perspective and situation on that unfortunate day, he reverted 'Joy you are my friend and whatever has happened has happened so let's bygone be bygone and let me know if you need any help from me.'

Pihu had also understood the situation of Joy after talking to Shree. Life has also taught her that good friendships are rare and one should take all the measures possible to preserve good friendship, so she repeated what Robi said that she would extend whatever help she can to make Durga pujo a big success.

Moloy looked at Sharad "Let bring back our friendship and let's get over this.

Shree tried to convince Sharad, ' Sharad, do you know your friend; he is not bad at heart.

Sharad replied 'He is good at heart, but he is stupid, he doesn't understand that even after assuming the reason for this meeting if I have come here, it is only to support him. Then he pulls Joy to give him a tight hug.'

Sharad looked mischievously at Joy. 'You know that I am an editor, right.'

Joy smiled back. 'Thank you for coming, my friend, and I am sorry once again for the miscommunication we had last time.'

Sharad whispered into his ears, 'You need not say sorry anymore; let's plan for the Durga pujo.'

They all sat along the stairway, dropping into the pond.

Joy continued 'We all wanted to do something different when we were children; Sharad wanted to change the system, Moloy wanted to pursue creative art, Pihu wanted to pursue music, Shree wanted to pursue dance, so let's use this opportunity to fulfil that dream. I am ready to take on the trolls if this Durga pujo is not judged as the best Durga pujo, but it should be a version of us. We should feel satisfied that we have given it our all and have enjoyed it to the fullest. I have something different in mind from my experience in Denmark. Let's start with dividing the responsibilities amongst us.'

After I went to see the town with Moloy a few days back, I realised that the Durga pujo which we are planning to arrange must bring some positive change into the life of the normal people. I can buy an expensive idol or spend a huge amount of money into decoration, but it would not yield any benefit for the people who are looking up to Durga Maa to do something for them.

'Will an event of a few days bring any long-lasting change in people's lives?' Robi was very sharp with his question.

Nobody said you can't, so there is no harm in trying,' Joy was quick to respond.

There was interim silence until everyone spoke in unison, 'Joy Maa Durga.'

Sharad poked Joy, 'Do you have any plan or.......?'

Joy has some rough sketches on a piece of paper, which he places in front of everyone.

He explained the plan in detail and divided the responsibilities between the friends. Joy and Moloy took the responsibility of the Goddess Durga idol and overall arrangement, Sharad took the responsibility of advertisement, Robi took the responsibility of making the food arrangements and lastly Pihu took the responsibility to arrange for cultural programmes and Shree took responsibility of the decorations.

They all were very much excited as they are going to do something together after a long, long time. They were sure to gather lots of sweet memories even if the Durga pujo doesn't turn out to be the best Durga pujo.

Would this Durga pujo complete the incomplete stories, unfinished aspirations and unspoken wishes or it will just add to it. It is to be seen, but for the time being let's praise Goddess Durga for bringing the friends together 'Joy Maa Durga.'

Drumbeats: Durga Pujo of Shantipur

Sharad was back to his daily routine of an editor. He must plan the advertising strategy of the Durga pujo. He found a letter on his table. It was from Nata Mallick, the general secretary of the largest and the most grand Durga Pujo of Kolkata. He had asked for a donation of ten lakhs rupees for the Durga pujo. Basically, it is not a request for donation but a disguised threat to donate the money or face dire consequences.

Now Sharad would have to talk to the board of directors and get the amount approved prior to donating the money to Nata Mallick.

Meanwhile Sharad had asked for his favourite portege Anand and Malobika. Every year they cover the news of Durga pujo for them so they are a well-known face in the world of Bengali media.

Sharad had already discussed in detail the advertising strategy with Joy and had set Joy in motion to complete some tasks in advance.

As per the plan, Sharad sent Malobika to Shantipur to build on the article in another newspaper about Joy claiming that the Durga Pujo of Shantipur will be the best Durga pujo this year, but this time, it will be from a different angle.

A few days later, there was an article in the newspaper about the Durga Pujo of Shantipur. It said that if you are bored and frustrated with the hustle and bustle of the city and want to enjoy the Durga Pujo in the Serenity of Shantipur, then here is the chance for you as there is an invitation from the heir of the zamindar of Shantipur. He had made a perfect arrangement with air-conditioned rooms and scope for indulging in extracurricular activities like pottery, painting, weaving, fishing, etc., besides being part of the best Durga pujo of the state as he has vowed that this year his Durga pujo would be the best Durga pujo.

It shared the link to the Facebook page of the Durga pujo arrangement.

If you go to the Facebook page then you will find different packages for different days, starting from one day to maximum 5 days from Shasti to Vijayadashami. It included everything from the moment you have reached Shantipur. But there were two limitations: first you needed to pay in advance according to the package you selected and secondly there was room for only 50 families.

It was a one-of-a-kind arrangement that was never thought of before. Since Malobika covered the news, it gave the required credibility to the news, and so soon, they started receiving lots of requests for the booking.

Meanwhile, before the article was published, Moloy and Joy worked with the slum dwellers to modify their rickshaws to the theme of Durga pujo. They had also been given traditional dress as uniforms so that they could be easily identified. Most of these rickshaw drivers were Muslim, but they agreed to do this as it would give them a chance to uplift the lives of their families in an honourable way.

Moloy and Joy had called in for a meeting with the villagers who were interested in supporting the arrangement of Durga pujo and discussed with them the idea of having a family as a guest during Durga pujo and getting paid a good amount of money for the same. A list of the people who had agreed to this idea was prepared, and their phone numbers were shared on the Facebook page.

Any family interested in joining the Durga pujo celebration had the option to talk to the owner of the available places before booking that for the celebration.

Joy would deduct some amount as a commission and fees for other services and the rest of the amount was transferred into the account of the respective resident receiving the guests.

Once a guest has made an online booking, then Shom, Praful's son, would coordinate with them on their mode and time of arrival at Shantipur. The specially modified rickshaw will then go to receive the guests with a small packet of complimentary sweets.

Robi, who had good insight into Bengali dishes, decided the menu for the guests for each day. The foods will be cooked in a single place and will then be distributed to the respective guests in tiffin boxes by young school-going kids who will get to earn little pocket money through this.

Shom gathered different entertainers like puppeteers, folk singers, and other artists from nearby villages to have different programmes during the day for the guests. He had also arranged for fishing in the ponds in different batches for those who would like to catch fish by themselves.

Moloy had planned a guided tour for the guests to the hand weaving shops of the famous Shantipuri Saree. This will give them insight into how clothes are woven and how different designs are copied on the sarees. They would also get a chance to buy sarees directly from the place where it is weaved at a much marginal rate compared to the air-conditioned shops in the cities.

Moloy and Joy arranged to put up temporarily erected shops and give on rent to local manufacturers of sculpture, local painting arts and locally manufactured ornaments like bangles and necklaces. This gave the opportunity to the people at the grassroots level to earn some money.

Meanwhile in Kolkata, Sharad was involved in an altercation with the board of directors of the newspaper firm on the topic of donation to Nata Mallick for the Durga pujo. Nata Mallick had been increasing the donation amount every year, and it has become a one-sided affair because of his political connections. The board of directors are upset with this arm-twisting by Nata Mallick. Probal Sen, who is one of the board members, categorically blasted Sharad.

Probal countered, 'We cannot allow this to happen year after year; we need to find a solution for this.'

'We need to gulp down this bitter pill, as Nata Mallick has political backing and would resort to negative publicity about the newspaper if we don't succumb,' replied Sharad.

Probal was more aggressive this time. 'But there has to be a way out...!!!!'

Sharad was quiet and in a contemplative state.

Probal reiterated, 'Am I speaking to a wall?'

Sharad was polite and firm this time. 'We need to create a competitor for him so that next time, he will be satisfied with whatever we give him.'

Probal replied, 'Good, then you look for the runner-up for last year's Durga pujo and sponsor some amount of money to them as well.'

Sharad immediately cut him off. 'No, we need to find a Durga pujo which is not famous at all and we need to make it look like that after our support that Durga pujo became famous.'

Probal Sen whispered slowly, 'Do you have something in mind?'

Yes, the son of a zamindar has vowed to win the prize for the best Durga pujo. Nata Mallick is also eyeing the same trophy, as this would be his third consecutive win, which has never happened in history. I think we should pit this zamindar with Nata Mallick.

Wonderful!!! Let's make it happen! Exclaimed Probal Sen.

Sharad subsequently made arrangements with Probal to sponsor the Durga pujo. Joy gave an interview as per agreement wherein he vociferously claimed the trophy of the best Durga pujo. The purpose was to make people interested in joining the event and instil some threat in the mind of Nata Mallick.

Soon, his interview appeared in the local newspaper and became a talking point for the town.

That means that Nata Mallick is aware of the situation and now and henceforth the game will be played in open air.

Stakes are higher for Nata Mallick and Sharad is aware of that. Sharad is looking for the opportunity to square off his revenge with Nata Mallick. Meanwhile, people in West Bengal have started gearing up for the Durga pujo; the shopping has started, the plannings are being made and the one common topic for gossip is 'Who will win the award for the best Durga pujo this time?'

Idol

Moloy and Joy had decided to get the Maa Durga idol from the Kumartully, so they planned a day trip to the place to pay the advance money and book the idol for Durga pujo. Kumartully is a place near Kolkata which is famous for sculpting beautiful idols of Maa Durga for Durga pujo.

The history of Kumartully dates to pre-independent India. When Britain colonised India, they established new villages around their capital at that time in India,i.e. Calcutta 1. The villages of Gobindapur, Sutanuti and Kalikata later merged into what we know today as modern-day Kolkata, previously Calcutta.

They had established different localities for people with specific skills. The prominent amongst them were Suriparah for wine dwellers, Collotolah for oil extractors, Chuttarparah for carpenters and Coomartuli for porters. Eventually, the porters in Coomartolly started making idols for worship and became experts in that. Now, it is known as Kumartully.

Presently all the major Durga pujo associations source their idols from Kumartully as it is made by the best artists of the trade.

This made Moloy and Joy decide to get the Maa Durga idol from Kumartully. It takes 3 hours to drive from Shantipur to Kumartully, so Moloy and Joy start early in the morning by car so that they reach Kumartully in good time.

Kumartully was filled with different circuitous lanes, and they could see different artists working on the idols with great precision. Joy could not help noticing the focus in their eyes when they were giving the final touch to the idols and secondly the fact that they were making the idols in bare top and lungi whereas the idols which they are making are draped in silk sarees. The idol cannot feel the difference between silk and cotton, which, ironically, human beings can.

Joy thought that the reason might be the same as why people give fewer flowers to other people than they offer to God: the fact that avoiding pain is usually the bigger motivator than getting pleasure, and people offer flowers to God as a gift for God to straighten things for them.

Joy asked one of the artisans how much he earns, and he replied that he earns 10,000 rupees. Then, he asked about the cost of the idol he was making, which he said was one lakh rupees. Considering the fact that he can work on 3-4 idols in a month, Joy quickly calculated that he was getting a meagre 2.5 % of the total revenue as a salary, which is also an approximate percentage of the revenue that an average company in India allocates for the salaries of its human resources. He thought to himself that the psychology of humans as a unit is a big contributing factor in building a bigger unit like a company and eventually a state and a nation.

There was mass production of the Maa Durga idol going on there, and Joy realised that if he purchased the Durga idol from there, then he would also become a contributor to the status quo. So, after roaming for 4 hours, looking at different idols, they decided to return to Shantipur without placing an order for the Maa Durga idol.

On their way back, Joy decided to visit the village temple to calm his mind and think of a way out of this situation. When he was in school he would often visit the temple in lure of the sugar candies which the priest Mr. Ashok Banerjee, lovingly called Pandit Babu, would happily give to all the attendees of the temple. He used to live in a small hutment near the temple, built by the villagers.

He had made a small farm near the hutment wherein he would grow vegetables and flowers required for worshipping God. Panditbabu had lost his wife to an endemic disease and was living with his only daughter, Rita. Rita is of marriageable age, but Pandit Babu is unable to find a suitable suitor for Rita as she has a dark complexion. She is meticulous in all household tasks like cooking, cleaning, washing clothes, etc., which a married woman is expected to do in a rural village, but just because of her complexion, she had been rejected many times.

Joy could see the priest from the distance as he was dozing off on the floor of the temple. Joy knelt to touch the feet of the priest to get his blessings. Panditbabu looked through the corner of his eyes and got energised to see Joy before his eyes. He was aware of the developments in the village over the Durga pujo topic. He assumed that Joy was there to request him to conduct the Durga pujo.

There was silence for a brief period until Pandit Babu started.

Pandit Babu said, 'So, how is the preparation for the Durga pujo going?'

Joy was silent and lost in his thoughts. He has very little time left for the Durga pujo and so many things to do. So, he was also mentally disturbed by what he saw in Kumartully.

Panditbabu stood up and returned with some sugar candies.

Panditbabu had a satirical tone while offering the sugar candies to Joy. 'Have this: sometimes you need to add sweetness to your life, so tell me what is wrong with you.'

Joy filled his mouth with the sugar candies and responded, 'I hope this works.'

Joy noticed that Panditbabu was still staring at him, expecting more to come, so Joy continued, we went to Kumartully today to buy Maa Durga idol, but it was frustrating to see the condition of the artists, so we decided not to buy the Durga idol from there, but then I realised that everywhere it is more of a business rather than genuine worship.

Panditbabu responded, 'I agree with you that nowadays it is more of a showoff with grandiloquent decorations and beautiful statues of Maa Durga rather than actual worship of Maa Durga, but you know things were not like this in the past.'

Pandit babu continued, there is a sculptor named Jahar Babu in our village. He used to make idols for all the pujo, such as Durga pujo, Kali pujo, and Saraswati pujo, for the village. Villagers used to pay him in cash or kind based on their capacity, and he would make idols for them based on their ability to pay.

It was a stable system that ensured everyone gets to enjoy the festival, not the fortunate few, however things have changed a lot since then.

Joy was patiently listening to Panditbabu, so Panditbabu thought of making an important point as well.

Pandit Babu heaves a sigh. 'Durga pujo is all about the celebration of Maa Durga's homecoming to her maternal home, i.e., earth, for a few days. These days, every sculptor is busy making Maa Durga look good and beautiful, but nobody thinks about the fact that Maa Durga mustn't necessarily look beautiful but obviously be compassionate and empathetic. Your girl is your girl even when she is not beautiful in the eyes of the world because, for you, she is always beautiful.'

The eyes of Pandit Babu were wet. He spoke with a heavy voice, 'This is the reason my daughter is not getting married off, even so she can do all the household chores meticulously.'

Joy was confused and he didn't know what to say or how to react but for sure he had a change of mind. Joy started thinking about Misti in the same context. He started to think that maybe Misti is a beautiful girl for him, but the world will judge her differently based on their own criteria.

Moloy broke the spell of silence. 'I can see your daughter getting married very soon. Don't worry; everything is done at the right time.'

Joy asked Moloy. Do you have Jahar Babu's address?

Moloy nodded yes.

They both touched the feet of Pandit Babu and asked him if he would agree to be the priest for the Durga pujo.

The enigmatic smile was back on Pandit Babu's face. 'Yes, of course. Don't worry about that.'

Moloy and Joy returned with a happy face. They have a priest for the pujo; now they just need to arrange an idol.

While in the car, Joy was contemplating the fact that 'Life is so beautiful if we just keep it simple and accessible to all. If we just create an environment where each one of us can be our true self, devoid of any bias of any kind.'

Joy has started appreciating the circular economy prevalent in the past that ensured that wealth is distributed across the different strata of society through the implementation of simple measures. But the challenge is that the villagers who were the foundation of such a well-oiled and functional system have given in to the comfort of immediate gratification and self-care. The smiling face of the neighbour is not important anymore.

Joy was thinking, 'Can old values be revived?'

Finance

Joy had the task of arranging the finances for the Durga pujo. Most of his concerns are already solved by Sharad by the arrangement of sponsorship, but it would not lead to the celebration of the essence of Durga pujo, which involves ushering in hope and light in the life of the people, inspiring everyone to separate out the wrong practices in the society and bring forth togetherness just as the swan that filters out milk from the water.

History has proved many times that luxury provided as a gift has never lasted long. Joy also wanted to bring back the essence of Durga pujo, which he used to enjoy in his childhood and which now just remains in the books of famous writers Sharadchandra and Bankimchandra.

Joy wanted to create a stream of income that would self-sustain the Durga pujo for years to come. So, he mapped all the different aspects related to Durga pujo.

Food	Emotional aspect
Egg Roll	Ambience
Mughlai	Music
Chicken Biryani	Dance and fun
Sweets	
Dress	**Decoration**
Traditional	Artistic
Colorful	Piece of art
Unique	

Joy decided to generate money from all these different aspects of the Durga pujo. This will not be easy because it ultimately needs to come out of the pockets of the people who are going to come from outside to attend the Durga pujo, and they should have a valid reason to pay.

Joy decided to integrate all these different aspects of the Durga pujo to create a new brand, i.e., Shantipur. Joy decided to build on the theory of exclusivity to make that possible.

Shantipur is known for its hand-weaved cotton sarees. Joy decided to utilise this fact to generate income. He ordered 500 sarees of white colour with red borders, which will be sold to all the women attending the Durga pujo. There is a speciality in these sarees. It would have 'Shantipur Durgotsav' written on its borders.

All the saree manufacturers who want to sell sarees to visitors need to register in advance with the Durga Pujo Committee by paying money and giving a 1-hour tour of their weaving facility. They will then be part of the walking tours arranged for the Durga pujo visitors.

He arranged a meeting with all the sweet shop owners to find a special sweet that could be linked to the image of Shantipur. Shantipur has a huge production of jack fruits. They tried different combinations to combine jackfruit with different sweet dishes, and at last, they successfully created a flavoured Rassagola, which is a sweet dessert.

Two important points were agreed upon with all the shopkeepers: they would sell these delicacies only during the Durga pujo, and secondly, they would contribute one rupee for each dessert sold for the Durga pujo. Initially, there was opposition, but later, they understood that considering the seasonal nature of the jack fruit and the size of the population of Shantipur, it would be more beneficial if they maintained this exclusivity and used this as a selling proposition to attract more visitors for the Durga pujo in the coming year.

Many small changes were made to have exclusivity rather than a contribution to the Durga pujo.

The base for the egg roll was made square rather than round. All the shopkeepers were advised to use brown edible colour in their chicken biryani to make their biryani look different with very little change in taste and chicken biryani was renamed as 'Shantipuri chicken biryani.'

Shree, being a software engineer, created a website for this event. All the visitors interested in attending this event need to register for the event and pay the registration fees. They would then receive an invite from the Shantipur village in their inbox.

The visitors will also receive a newsletter on things to do, places to visit and food joints, along with discount coupons. They would stay in Shantipur with a local family who would serve them with generous hospitality and would take care of their well-being.

Visitors have the opportunity to advance book value added services like boat ride, fish catching adventure, kite flying experience, walking tour to the temples etc.

A small training course in local arts and music was also arranged for the people interested.

Aged people of Shantipur were given training in storytelling so that they could keep the children engaged while their parents enjoyed the pujo.

T-shirts were printed with Shantipur Durga pujo brand, which was in line with the overall theme of the event.

Joy has made electronic transfer mandatory for registering for the event so as to have clear accountability of cash flow and expenditures.

Everything seemed to be meticulously planned and provisioned, but everyone missed one key aspect of this equation.

They underestimated the demand for such a concept, so they went full throttle on advertising the event in all types of media with the help of Sharad.

Soon, in no time, all the registration places were full. Now, there were phone calls for registering for the event, and subsequently, warnings started pouring in that they would not allow this event to happen if they were not allowed there.

This was something that was not planned, and Joy didn't had any idea how to handle this situation.

It has been rightly said that two kinds of people are cursed: first, who have too little and second, who have too much.

Joy had to find the means to manage additional requests for registration.

The last few days were really tiring for Joy because of aggressive and extensive planning and coordination work, so Joy decided to sleep a little late the next day.

As he woke up the next day, he could hear Maa telling the story of a thirsty crow to Misti from Panchatantra. Panchatantra is a book which uses fictional animal characters to impart teaching of human values. It had been written by sages long back and has been transferred from generation to generation through word of mouth before it has been written down and translated into different languages.

In previous days there used to be excellent storytellers that used to roam around the village telling stories in exchange for fistful rice or grains.

Maa was telling Misti how the thirsty crow saw a slender earthen pot with little water and, rather than giving it up, collected small pebbles from nearby places and used it to fill the pot till water came on the top so that he could drink it. Maa was trying to emphasise the importance of grit to Misti.

Joy overheard the conversation between Maa and Misti in his half-sleep. It gave him a fresh lease of energy. He vowed to find a solution to this problem.

He thought of paying a visit to Dakshineswar temple to pay his regards to Goddess Kali and request for showing the way.

Dakshineswar temple is considered to be one of the celebrated temples of Goddess Kali. One interesting fact about the temple is that across India, we would find many temples or monuments that are built by rich men or zamindars, but the Dakshineswar temple was built by a lady named Rani Rashmoni. This temple was further made famous by its priest, Ramakrishna Paramhansa, and decorated orator and speaker, Swami Vivekananda.

As per tradition Joy had observed fast that day. Normally devotees observe fast before offering their prayers to Goddess Kali and then they enjoy the delicious fried flat bread (kochuri) and Daal in the shops surrounding the temple.

Joy followed the same custom and offered his prayers while fasting. Subsequently, he went to the shops to enjoy delicious kochuri. Joy has a habit of entering into conversations with people.

Joy saw a lean boy cladded in cotton cloth serving him the kochuri, so he initiated the talk.

Joy queried, 'How much do you earn every day?'

Boy replied with a smile: 50 rupees and hundreds of smiles.

Joy got curious, so he further asked, 'With money, it is clear that every day you are being paid a percentage of the sale or an agreed amount as a sale. What about the smiles? How do you earn it?'

Boy replied, 'It is easier than earning money. You see, everybody comes here to ask for something from the Goddess Kali; they do so even when they donate money to poor beggars. I simply tell them that I have this intuition that their wish will be granted.'

Joy was amused by the intelligence of a young boy who looked very ordinary. While the boy served Joy water, he asked about his name: 'What is your name?'

Boy replied, 'I am called Abdul in this world.'

Joy immediately responded, 'You are a Muslim. Don't hesitate to work in a Hindu worshipping place.'

Boy was unperturbed; he said, 'God is one; what is the problem if you call it by one name and I by another? I am just trying to better my life, which is given by the same God, by ethical means.'

Joy realised his mistake, so he tried to correct his stand. 'You are right, young boy. I was just checking your point of view.'

While Joy was responding back to Abdul, he realised that adjacent to Shantipur, there was another village, Rasulgarh, populated mainly by the Muslim community. Though they are Muslim, their cultural differences are very minor. They even celebrate Durga pujo which is a Hindu tradition though in a small way.

It struck Joy's mind that if he could convince the villagers of Rasulgarh to join hands with them, they could register more people.

It would also accentuate the secularity of the magnanimous country of India.

Joy had a smile on his face and hope in his heart now. He stood up and gave his wholehearted regards to Abdul.

Joy said: 'Abdul, you are a true follower of one God. Keep doing your good deeds.'

Joy then decided to return back to Shantipur immediately and approach the head of the Rasulgarh village Muhammad Rehman with his proposal.

Joy went to Rasulgarh village the very next day to discuss his proposal with Muhammad Rehman.

Rehman was a short guy with lean composure. He was in his late fifties and was very soft-spoken, though short with words. Most of the time, he was nodding his head sparingly in agreement or disagreement to save revealing his thoughts.

Joy started the discussion by enquiring about the village.

Joy: 'I have passed through this village many times on my journey to Kolkata; however, only this time have I been fortunate enough to spend some quality time here. What are the grains that you cultivate in this village?'

Muhammad: We have just harvested potatoes, and in November, we will start sowing rice.

Durga pujo normally happens in the month of October, when one harvesting season is over and the next sowing season is yet to start. This gives people time to enjoy the festival before they start to get their hands dirty again.

Joy enquired, 'then most of the villagers must be comparatively free now; how are they engaging themselves?'

Muhammad replied, 'there is a brick factory two villages later, most of them are working as temporary labourer there.'

Joy mentioned, 'It's a pity that they don't get to spend some well-deserved spare time with their family.'

Mohammad affirmatively nodded.

Joy could see the house of Mohammad decorated with lights, so he curiously enquired.

Joy: 'It seems you have a marriage in your family.'

Mohammad again nodded affirmatively.

Robi's sweet shop in Shantipur is well-known in that region, so Joy decided to extend a helping hand here.

Joy mentioned, 'I would like to help you here; I will get you a highly discounted price for the wedding sweets from the sweet shop in Shantipur.'

Mohammad spoke now, 'Is that the reason for your visit?'

Joy realised that he should not be beating around the bush anymore, so he explained his plan of involving them in this year's Durga pujo celebration.

Joy further added 'There had been sparring communal riots between two communities in the past, maybe this will give us an opportunity to understand each other better and avoid such unpleasant episodes in future.'

This will also lead to the generation of better income for the villagers at home rather than working in a factory as a temporary labourer.

Mohammad patiently listened to all the arguments by Joy and then responded wisely, 'this should not be a one man's decision, so let me talk to my community, and I will get back to you.'

Few days later Mohammad sent the message that he could convince the villagers to participate in the Durga pujo since it involved generation of better income for them.

So, temporary huts were built in the Rasulgarh village for the additional people who were interested in joining the pujo. All the people who had expressed their interest to join the Durga pujo event, besides confirmed registration, were sent confirmation, and subsequently, registration details were removed from the website.

Before the term religion was invented, there was only one dharma and that was humanity. There were differences but they were celebrated, not frowned upon. Sometimes in the wake of preserving our culture we shatter the basic foundation of our existence and that is humanity.

God, in whatever form we preach, loves all of us equally and wants us to live harmoniously together, and that might be the reason for such a turn of events.

Mahalaya

Mahalaya holds a special place in the heart of all the Bengalis. It normally takes place 7 days before the start of Durga pujo from Panchami (which is a Sanskrit word for 5th). Mahalaya marks the end of Pitru Paksha which is the time for offering water to the ancestors. It is said in Hindu tradition that people get converted into an ethereal state when they die, and they eagerly wait for their heir to offer them water during Pitru Paksha.

When these traditions were established, the purpose must have been to establish a time in the year when everyone would remember their ancestors and learn good and bad lessons from their life, but it instead propagated malice like female feticide in society, as girls were not allowed to offer water to their ancestors. As it is said, 'success of any plan lies in its executor;' you can bring out corrupt practices even from the best rules established for the best interest of the society.

Mahalaya is also considered a day of invocation as it marks the advent of Maa Durga with her children into this mortal world.

Normally the day starts with the invocation of the Chandi path, i.e., shlokas of Maa Durga recorded by Birendra Krishna Bhadra. This is the time when everyone tunes in to the Radio to listen to the early morning telecast of the shloka (Chandi path) by Radio Broadcasting. This gives a sense of the beginning of the Durga pujo.

By this time, the Durga Pujo of Shantipur had become a big news. Sharad utilised his capacity as an editor of a leading newspaper to ensure that all the unique activities related to the Durga pujo in Shantipur were described in detail in the newspaper.

On top of it, Joy got his Danish friends to come to see the Durga Pujo of Shantipur, which is also getting media coverage. Joy had generously arranged for the accommodation of the journalists visiting Shantipur to cover the Durga pujo event and ensured that they got special hospitality. In turn they were going gung-ho over all the activities taking place there.

Joy had instructed all the villagers not to listen to the Chandi path in their home in isolation but to assemble outside his bungalow. He had made a dais beside his bungalow. It is always more enjoyable when you enjoy good moments together.

All the journalists were surprised to find all the people coming in hordes to assemble outside the bungalow of Joy. They also followed them to see the reason for the same.

As the clock ticked 6, a sweet voice started reciting the shloka of Maa Durga, also called Chandi path. The voice was coming from behind the dais. Soon, Pihu walked up the stage, reciting the shlokas in rhythm. These shlokas are written in Sanskrit and describe the beauty and quality of Maa Durga and how she wards off the evil intentions of Mahishasura on her.

Shloka are the couplets that describe a scene in the complete story. The Chandi path ultimately ends with Maa Durga killing Mahishasura with her sword.

Pihu was chanting the shloka so meticulously that everyone present there was taken by awe. She was so engaging that the audience was feeling the pain, desperation and anger instilled in the shloka as she was chanting it.

Soon, she started reading the last couplets, which were when the fight between Mahishasura and Maa Durga started.

Shree was standing beside the stage making the hand and face movements as Pihu was reciting the shloka, as there is a dance version as well to tell the same story. The dancers use their facial expressions to express the sorrow and anger of Maa Durga, as different voice intonations are used by a singer. She was feeling the urge to express herself as she is a trained dancer.

Soon, she felt a hand on her head. It was Praful Kaku.

Praful said.' I am like your father, and I am saying go and perform. Don't restrain yourself. Set yourself free.

As Pihu starts reading the shloka, where Maa Durga gets filled with anger and decides to fight with Mahishasura herself, Shree enters the stage with a wooden sword in her hand, impersonating Maa Durga. Her hairs were loosened out, her eyes red with anger, and her gait was filled with infatuation. She was reflecting the anger that any woman would have when she realised that this society cannot protect her and that she needs to protect herself.

The audience was dazzled at such an impeccable combination of perfect recitation and a perfect dance.

In the final couplet when Mahishasura resurfaces to attack Maa Durga, everyone stood up in excitement, though they all have heard and seen such performances before but this one was so different. Their mouths were wide open in tension as if they didn't know what would happen.

Just then, Praful enters the stage, impersonating Mahishasura with a wooden sword in his hand. He advances toward Shree, impersonating Maa Durga with a huge roar and anger. But he cannot walk properly without a wooden stick because of his age and pain in his knee, so as he walks towards Shree in anger, he falls on his knee. He raises his sword to kill Shree, impersonating Maa Durga, but she puts her left foot on the shoulder of Praful and imitates inserting the trident on his chest, signifying the victory of Maa Durga over Mahishasura and good over evil. The curtain falls. Shree starts crying as soon as she comes out of the character of Maa Durga, as she has kept her feet on her kaku, whom she treats just like her father.

Praful gets up and consoles her with a smile. 'You should be a proud daughter as you have killed the devil inside me.'

Joy comes rushing back to the stage. He was awestruck by Shree's dance.

Joy poked her. 'I didn't expect you to have such a good hold on dance still now, as I have never seen you dancing often in Denmark.'

Shree replied,' Dance is a language of expression of your body. It comes naturally. She looked at Praful kaku and continued, 'When it comes, just let it flow, don't restrain it.

Joy and Shree also congratulated Pihu for her splendid recitation of shloka. It had instilled a new confidence in her. She realised that the old Pihu was somewhere still well preserved within her and was just waiting for an opportunity to spurt out.

Joy said to Pihu again,' Pihu, I am really sorry, I was not there to save you when you required your friends the most. I could have saved you from getting married so early but I went into hibernation and didn't know that your world was turning upside down behind my back.

Sometimes you regret your actions so much that saying sorry multiple times makes you feel lighter.

Later, what happened was not anticipated by anyone, at least not to the magnitude it had acquired. All the news channels were going berserk with the continuous telecast of the programme. Pihu and Shree had become celebrities. Some news channels even interviewed them to understand how they came up with such a wonderful idea.

There were two key people watching their interview with keen interest. One was Nata Mallick, the general secretary of the most famous Durga pujo committee of Kolkata, that had won the award for the best Durga pujo for consecutive two years now and it needs to win this year to be the first ever Durga pujo committee to have won the award for three consecutive year.

Second was Deep, yes, the same boy who wanted to express his love for Pihu and followed her to the ladies toilet.

After the unfortunate incident at school, Deep was in mental trauma, as he knew within him that he had done wrong by spreading rumours about Joy and Pihu, but Indian society seldom forgives somebody who accepts his mistake, so he kept everything within himself. He saw Pihu getting married to a much older guy, which made him sink even deeper into remorse. He was feeling guilty, and unfortunately, cascading events were set into motion, and it didn't stop until it claimed its bounty.

He started resorting to smoking weed and taking alcohol to forget that incident, but it didn't leave him for a moment. At last, he found solace in drama, wherein he found a stage to be somebody he was not, to vent out his frustration and vulnerability.

Gradually he became successful and moved to Mumbai for acting in films. He didn't get a chance to act in films but gradually with his hard work and dedication he became one of the best directors of Bollywood. He had forgotten everything with the passage of time until he saw the interview of Pihu in the news channel telling the importance of Mahalaya.

It would be important to see how he influences the future course of the story.

Meanwhile in Shantipur, Joy went to take bath in Ganga, which is a pious river as per Hindu mythology. He worshipped his ancestors and offered his prayers to them. As he turned around after taking dips in Ganga, he heard the voice of his grandfather Protap Mukherjee talking to him in his same disciplinarian accent but with a mild tone.

Protap Mukherjee said, 'Now you are acting like my grandchild, and I am sure that you will soon relieve me from the curse of daily shaming on the hand of Sukanto Mukherjee here in heaven. Go for it. Make their family repay with interest. Then there was a brief silence until that voice started speaking again.' You know why I failed because I was not connected with my people. I wanted my people to win the football match without knowing what will encourage them to win it. Life had taught me that you get exceptional results when you also enjoy the process instead of channelling all your energy into just winning. There must be a purpose much bigger than just winning. You need to ensure that you don't fall into the same trap.

Protap Mukherjee spoke again after brief silence 'I had built this bungalow with 15 rooms not because I wanted everyone to live together happily but to have many people obeying my orders. That led to people gradually drifting apart and now ten rooms in my bungalows are locked. So, if your purpose is pure, you will definitely succeed.'

Joy briefly looked down, contemplating, and he found no one when he looked up again.

Durga pujo festivity is going to start soon, and Joy can feel the presence of the divine deities around, the message through the spirit of Protap Mukherjee is just a sign that he will be looked after if his purpose is pure.

Will Joy fall to the rush in emotions and impulse of winning the prize of best Durga Puja or will he now just let it pass.

Taking people together in your journey is always difficult, it is always challenging when you need to consider so many views, have so many arguments before taking a simple decision, but it's beautiful when you have many people celebrating your success. Let's see what approach Joy takes now

Decoration

Decoration is an important aspect of any Durga pujo. Every year, you will find different pujo associations coming up with different innovative decoration concepts to attract people to see their idols. It's not uncommon to hear that some pujo Pandals have made replicas of famous monuments like the Taj Mahal or Birla temple as their pujo Mandal. It's like a race, and each pujo association tries different ways to outdo each other.

Decoration plays an important role in the judgement of the particular Durga pujo as exceptional or normal.

Joy was very sure that he cannot compete in this aspect with big Durga pujo associations with huge inflow of capital from different corporate sponsors. He needs to find a clever means to make the decoration of his Durga pujo an exceptional one. Just like any human being, Joy also had his sets of limitations and in this case his limitation was the lack of inclination towards art and craft.

Fortunately, Shree was inclined towards art and craft since her childhood. She would make beautiful sculptures from clay; pen stands from coconut leaves besides having a lot of interest in classical dance.

If Shree had her way, she would have never left India to go abroad, as she was very well connected with the roots and the rhythm of the country.

Since these types of art and craft is not that popular in Europe, she applied her energy in learning Origami and Painting which is very popular there.

She had jumped at the mention of Durga pujo decoration, and She had volunteered to plan for the Durga pujo decorations but the buy in from others were not smooth.

Robi, Moloy, Joy and Pihu were excited the moment they heard from Shree that she would take responsibility for the decoration. But there was blankness in Sharad's eyes.

His face subsequently was filled with a sarcastic smile that everybody noticed soon.

Joy enquired, 'What happened, Sharad?'

Sharad replied while looking in different direction, trying to avoid eye contact with Joy 'we have broadcasted everywhere that we will celebrate the best Durga pujo this year and we are just assembling amateurs here, I think it is matter of few days before we all get publicly criticised for our misadventures.'

Sharad continued, 'I will arrange for an adept artist from Kolkata, and he will make all the decorations behind the scenes, and we will tell everyone that we have made it; you leave that to me.'

There was silence in the group, and Shree felt embarrassed for taking the initiative to decorate.

Joy broke the silence 'how long we would live in the fear of the parents, of society, of peers, of success and failure. I think we should shift our focus from what we would lose to what we would gain, and I see that we would regain our inner pride if we arranged everything ourselves rather than getting it outsourced.'

Joy continued 'though our lives are long, there are only a few moments that make life worth living and this is one such occasion. Think what will happen if we win.'

Sharad was silent; he was not objecting, but there was also not acceptance from his side.

Robi and Moloy showed their support to Shree as they have identified the creative side of Shree during the previous meeting, through conversation. Pihu supported Shree as she very well knew how difficult it is for a woman to fetch a chance to lead in this world.

Joy was always there for Shree.

After everyone left, Joy whispered in the ears of Shree 'Sharad is a good guy, he will help you a lot if you can earn his trust, I have done my part now,you need to seize the moment.'

Shree inherent nature is that of an executor, so she keeps complete focus on the task at hand it is is completed.

She started planning for the decoration from the very next day.

Shree is an avid reader, so they went through different kinds of books to identified concepts for the Durga pujo decoration.

But whenever she would find a good concept, she would eventually discover that it has already been implemented in the previous Durga pujo somewhere.

Bengalis are considered to be very creative when it comes to arts and crafts, and that was making things very difficult for Shree, and she needed to find a unique concept for the Durga pujo.

While trying to find a good theme for the Durga pujo, she stumbled upon the fact that the Bengali calendar was developed during the reign of emperor Shashanka, who was the first emperor to establish the polity of unified Bengal.

She got curious so tried to find more information through different books and archaeological articles, however very little information was available in any forum.

After 2-3 days of strenuous search, she called for another meeting of the team. Since Sharad was considered to be the most well-informed person in the group, she started the meeting by asking an interesting question to Sharad.

Shree: 'Sharad, may I please ask you an interesting question about King Shashanka?'

Sharad: I will answer your question rightaway. King Shashanka ruled Bengal from 590 CE to 626 CE, and the Bengali calendar was established during his reign, he is also known as somebody who drove Buddhist monks out of Bengal.

Shree smiled. 'Thanks for the answer, though I was about to ask different question.' My question was, 'Do we know how the people of Bengal used to dress and eat, and what were their different occupations during the reign of King Shashanka?'

Sharad was silent, he knew in which direction things were moving. He asked for a daytime to revert.

The next day, he called Shree to confirm that very little information was available on King Shashanka, which included just a few gold and silver coins excavated from Rajbaridanga. However, he has organized a meeting with the archaeologist, Mr Banerjee, who led the excavation of the site.

This meant that Shree would have to paint a portrayal of an ancient civilisation based on the impression of an archaeologist.

Decoration

It's a pity how badly we treat our ancient heritage, however Shree had found her idea and that is to bring to life the glorious past of King Shashanka who had made significant contributions to the culture and heritage of West Bengal but somehow got lost in ignominy.

Dr Banerjee lives off the pension alone in a small house on the outskirts of Kolkata. His children live in Pune. Since he frequently lived away from his family in remote places, he faltered in developing a bond with his children. So, when his wife expired, he preferred to stay alone rather than stay with his children. Also, he was not ready to move out of West Bengal at this fag end of his life.

Shree and Sharad had a meeting with Dr. Banerjee, the famous archaeologist. Since this topic was very close to his heart, Dr Banerjee spoke at length, and the meeting, which was supposed to be for one hour, lasted six hours, with a lunch break where Shree cooked lunch for Dr Banerjee and Sharad.

Sharad requested Dr Banerjee to visit Shantipur to see the decoration and promised that he will send a car for him.

It would be interesting to see how Shree incorporates her dialogue with Dr Banerjee into the decoration concepts and whether it reminds people about the rich culture of West Bengal or not.

Shasti

Shasti marks the first day of the five-day celebration. This is the day when the face of Maa Durga is unveiled before all. This is also the day when the Durga pujo arrangement is opened for the public to see.

All the outstation participants had already reached Shantipur yesterday. They were well received by the allocated local family members at the railway stations in the uniform finalised by the Durga pujo committee. In the station itself, they were handed over the memorabilia, dress for the events as per their registration and the full event calendar.

The excitement on the face of all the participants was very much visible. Wheelchairs were arranged for all the aged persons as required to make them comfortable. Just outside the station, one of the local residents was reciting local songs with ektara reinforcing the pujo environment already created.

There were many educated and big officials who had turned up for the event.

Since the number of participants exceeded their expectations, arrangements were also made in Rasulpur village. All were mesmerised by the unity in Diversity portrayed by the villagers of Shantipur and Rasulpur.

Among the participants there were colleagues of Nata Mallick, the president of the most famous Durga pujo in Kolkata. He would not leave any stone unturned that would impact his chances of winning the award for the best Durga pujo. The purpose of those people was to create issues and bring out the shortcomings of the arrangements to the fore.

In the morning, all the participants were woken up by Durga Vandana which is a song sung in praise of Goddess Durga. They all got ready in the dress given to them as a part of the welcome package and reached the location of the Durga pujo.

At the entry of the Durga pujo, there was a booth with headphones that explained the life of King Shashanka and his contribution to Bengali culture. This was done to condition all the Durga pujo participants about the context of decoration.

All of them were given some coins made in clay as was used in King Shashanka' s period in exchange of Indian currency and any purchase they make of the artefact inside the Durga pujo premises will be through these clay coins.

All the people were astounded by sheer simplicity, yet magnanimity of the decoration made by Shree. Press reporters were observing and taking pictures of the minor detail that has been cleverly and adeptly incorporated by Shree.

All the press reporters were so impressed by the decoration that they immediately called for Shree. They took her interview, asking how she zeroed in on this concept. Sharad had seen Shree's hard work, and now he was ensuring that she gets her share of recognition.

Anjan Ghosh the famous designer, who have also designed and decorated the Durga pujo mandap of Nata Mallick was watching the live broadcast of the event. He was also amazed at the concept and decided to visit Shantipur himself. He is a person in late 60s with a sheer eye for creativity.

Meanwhile, inside the mandap, Panditbabu had already started the invocation prayer to invite Maa Durga to the earthly abode. The next step is to complete the Bodhan pujo and unveil the face of Maa Durga. The incessant drumming of the dhak and ringing of the bells had turned the moment divine, the wait of a year is soon going to be consummated into the first sight of Maa Durga.

Soon Pandit babu completed the Bodhan pujo and hinted his assistant to take off the veil from Maa Durga's face. Johor Babu, the sculptor of the Maa Durga idol, was getting impatient now. He has risked his life in trying something new and if things don't go well then, he may get killed for hurting the religious sentiments of the people.

As soon as the veil was taken off, there was utter silence in place of joy and happiness. The sheer dismay was evident in the eyes of all the worshippers. Maa Durga had the dark complexion, and she had white spots on her face.

As an immediate reaction, participants started asking for return of their participation fees. The spies sent by Nata Mallick immediately came into action. They asked for the sculptor and took sticks in their hand to destroy all the decorations using this opportunity. All of this is getting covered through live media with people across the state watching it.

> *If nobody intervenes now, then everything will be lost.*

Meanwhile, Sharad could identify the rogues from the Nata Mallicks gang as they used to visit his office to collect money.

Suddenly, there was a huge shout from behind. It was Maa.

The dominance and sharpness of a Zamindari family was evident in her voice.

Maa said firmly 'You are free to do whatever you want, we would return your money as well if that's what you want but first listen to the reasoning from Joy, why Maa Durga is like this.'

Since all of this was live telecasted, Nata Mallick was having the laugh of his life. He was unable to recollect when he had laughed like this in the past.

In the meantime, Sharad, with the help of Moloy, Robi and other villagers, quietly took out the goons from Nata Mallick's gang from the crowd so that they don't interrupt when Joy is explaining the rationale to them.

All these goons were very ferocious in their young days and were very instrumental in establishing the influence of Nata Mallick however over a period of time they lost that edge and have been capitalizing on the past impressions. That day they got so badly beaten up by the local villagers that they were praying that hopefully they would not have to pay interest for their past sins.

Here inside the mandap Joy requested 5-6 women to come on the stage. All these women had a white spot in different parts of their face. They had a slightly dark complexion just like Maa Durga.

Joy said 'These white spots come from malnourishment and having high content of arsenic in the drinking water. The villagers have been requesting the government for a long time to put a water filtration unit in the village, but nobody has been acting on it. How would we keep Maa Durga beautiful if we don't take care of her?'

There was silence, many people live two parrallel life, they paint a dream which is perfect and make them forget about the harsh reality and then in their real life they become ignorant to work on the improvement of their life to make it similar to their dream. Maa Durga is part of their dream,that needs to be perfect. Joy has shattered their frame of mind and compelled them to accept the reality and work toward improving the reality. Gradually, Maa, Sharad, Shree joined Joy in explaining to all the guest about the motive behind this and the elaborate arrangements made for them so that they have the best time of their life. Gradually things were back to normal and the first hurdle was successfully crossed.

Panditbabu started the amontron (invocation) pujo procedure as per the norm which are the mantras to invite the soul of Maa Durga into the idol.

Meanwhile the news had spread that Shantipur doesn't have clean drinking water and the cabinet minister had already sent a show cause notice to the local MLA on why the fund allocated for this purpose was not used in the right place.This has further increase the visibility of the Shantipur Durga pujo.

After the Shasti pujo, all the pujo participants had free time, so they decided to utilise their coupons. Some went to the sweet shop of Robi, and others went to see the weavers factory of Moloy. Since there was a special sweet created for them only for this purpose people just went overboard in enjoying that. There was a huge sale, so, revenue spiked like never before.

In the weaver's factory, people got to weave small parts themselves which they enjoyed a lot. Moloy had also created displays of many sarees from which visitors bought sarees as per choice.

All the children were left with local grandmothers who would keep them engaged with folk stories and native board games.

There was so much to do for everyone that people were spoilt for choices.

Pihu was responsible for the cultural programme. Cultural programmes were organised in the evening in the open ground like it used to happen in early days. People would make a circle around the artists and the artists would perform wholeheartedly in the centre. There was no distinction between people and when the artists used to complete their play they were filled with applause from all directions to the content of their heart.

Shree had knowledge that people have started enjoying Karaoke, so she had arranged for visitors to sing with the live local instrument's players. There was huge spurge in status update of the visitors in Facebook and Instagram with #Shantipur Durga Pujo.

Since tomorrow is going to be another day filled with lots of activities, all the people were served dinner at 8:30 pm so that all can go to sleep by 9:30 pm and come fresh for the scores of activities for tomorrow.

> *It was a once in a lifetime experience for many people as this was the first time they have come out of a city and got introduced to the rich cultural heritage. They were surprised by the open-heartedness and generosity of the villagers, where guests are still treated as God as the saying goes "Atithidevo bawa".*

Saptami

Saptami is the seventh day of Navratri. This is the day when you attend Maa Durga like a father. The pujo ceremony starts with infusing life into the idol of Maa Durga. Panditbabu diligently chanted mantras with different hand postures, inviting Maa Durga to make her presence in the idol. There are mantras where you assume giving life to different parts of Maa Durga.

Magically, after the infusion of life into Maa Durga idol, you can feel the difference. You can sense the happiness that a woman feels when she comes to her maternal home.

Then, there is the procedure of offering the stems of nine types of fruit-bearing plants to Maa Durga. These include the banana plant (represents goddess Bhramani), colocasia/Kochu in Bengali (represents goddess Kalika), turmeric plant (represents Goddess Durga), Jayanti tree (goddess Karthiki), wood apple tree/bilva/bel (goddess Shiva, another name for Goddess Durga), pomegranate tree (goddess Raktadantika), Ashoka (goddess Sokrahita), Arum plant/maan kochu in Bengali (goddess Chamundi) and rice plant/dhaan (goddess Maha Lakshmi. They represent different forms of Maa Durga and signify the fact that after the killing of Mahishasura, the balance had been reestablished by Maa Durga, and hence, vegetation flourished.

Subsequently there was arrangement for the bath of Maa Durga. It is an elaborate procedure, and you bathe her with around ten types of water, starting from water from pious river Ganges, rainwater, silver water, gold water etc. Subsequently you bathe her with milk, yogurt, honey to clean her and then again with water.

The underline is that you ensure the best of everything for Maa Durga. Then the offering of clothes, ornaments and cosmetics are done to ensure that she is happy and dresses up really well.

Her accompaniment Lord Ganesh, Goddess Lakshmi, Lord Kartik, and Goddess Saraswati are also offered similar gifts to make them happy and feel welcome.

Once they are ready in their new dresses and after taking a bath, they are offered food, which includes fruits, Khichuri, sweets of different kinds, and Indian dessert payasam.

Normally people fast till they offer flowers to Maa Durga. After food is offered, the priest arranges for Pushpanjali which is the act of offering flowers while praising and appreciating her presence and her qualities.

Subsequently fire is offered while praising Maa Durga and her accompaniment for their valour, kindness, and generosity. This is called aarti.

Considering the fact that fire has played a major role in propagation of human civilisation and guarding our existence from our predators it is considered to be an important offering.

We need to appreciate the fact that in earlier days fire could not be produced as easily as it is done today. Fire was protected with life and bartered with valuables when it was very difficult to spark a fire.

All the devotees are by now totally quenched in the festivities of Durga pujo. It was a normal scene to see someone abruptly starting to sing a devotional song or a poem. They all were really happy to enjoy their childhood kind of Durga pujo after a long time.

Robi had organised a competition of eating Indian delicacy Rassagola which are sweet balls made of fresh paneer and dipped in sugar syrup. There was a participation fee and a gift hamper for the winner.

The videos of different participants were recorded and posted on Facebook and Instagram with tag of #Shantipur Durga Pujo. There were many likes and comments. The winner of the competition won by a narrow margin by eating 150 Rassagola. Unfortunately, he had to be carried back to his place, since he was unable to move after eating 150 Rassagola.

Some news channels even artificially added to the news that it is a national record, which was later proved to be not true.

Meanwhile Anjan Ghosh, the famous designer who designs the pandals for Nata Mallick also reached Shantipur to check the decoration work with his own eyes. Since he was famous, the press was also covering him.

There was speculation that he would rip apart the decoration in Shantipur by identifying the lacunas. When Shree got to know of his presence in the pandal she was also more worried than happy. She was happy that Anjan Ghosh had come to see her work, but more worried just because of the irony of the situation.

But she still went to meet him. As she touched Anjan Ghosh's feet, he pulled her up and told her to make some tea for him.

While Shree was making the tea, she could hear Anjan Ghosh answering questions from the press reporters.

Press reporters: 'What is your view about the decoration work here?'

Anjan Ghosh replied: 'It is exceptional, just imagine a woman who doesn't have a formal education in arts and is staying abroad for a few years now, comes to India for a few days and comes up with such a wonderful concept. It is beyond imagination.'

Anjan Ghosh was sure that he would pay a high price to Nata Mallick because of such audacity, but he was an artist, and he perfectly understood what genuine appreciation means for an artist.

When the press reporters were gone, and Shree came with the tea, he explained different decoration concepts and correlations and also pointed out some areas of improvement for the future.

Shree thought that surely humbleness is one of the exceptional qualities of all high achievers.

Assessors of the best Durga pujo competition have been assessing all the competing Durga pujos every day. Previously, all the participating Durga pujo were within the main cities of Kolkata; only this year, Durga pujo of an outskirt area had dared to compete with them. This is simply because Durga pujo associations in the outskirts cannot even imagine having access to the funds that the Durga pujo associations in proper Kolkata city can have because of proximity to big corporate houses.

Two days have passed and the Shantipur Durga pujo is not featured even in the top five, even after huge appreciation showered on them by different streams of media.

Nata Malik's Durga pujo was leading the tally because of frequent visits of celebrities to his Durga pujo.

Deep, one of the co-students of Joy, Pihu, Robi and Sharad, the person who was responsible for the falling apart of friendship of Joy with his friends and who is now a celebrated director in Mumbai was closely following the progress in the media.

He realised that now the time has come up for him to visit Shantipur again, something he had been avoiding for years.

Meanwhile, in Shantipur, at night, musical events were organised by the local singers. It was done with the intention of providing a stage and media exposure to them. Some of the singers sang so beautifully that they were invited later to participate in the state level musical competition.

All the devotees were very happy with the arrangements and the way they were spending their days in Shantipur.

However, when it came to the ranking, Shantipur Durga Pujo was way behind.

Since children were spending time with the elderly people of the village where they were told about good habits and previous customs, they were sharing them with their parents later. This way parents were happy that their children are getting to know old customs which were part of their life.

Cultural programmes were completed by 8:00 p.m. as usual so that all the devotees can go to sleep by 9:30 pm after dinner.

Next day is the biggest day i.e., Ashtami and still Shantipur are nowhere near the top of the competition.

Ashtami

Ashtami is considered to be the most auspicious day of the Durga pujo. It is the day; it is believed that Maa Kali appeared from the forehead of Maa Durga and killed the demons named Chanda munda and Raktabija who were accompanying the demon Mahishasura.

The Ashtami pujo started early in the morning as per plan. It is the day when most of the people fast to offer flowers to Goddess Durga.

This is also the day when small girls who are in their pre-puberty age are worshipped as a symbol of Maa Durga.

It had always been the tradition or custom to respect girls and this had been nicely woven into different religious customs. However, problems started happening when people with their vested interest ignored the essence of the traditions in real day to day life.

Sharad had come with a wonderful idea where in the list of all the girls who are studying in small classes and are finding it difficult to study because of lack of money were broadcasted in the screen and people had the opportunity to make even small contributions to help these girls continue their study.

Once a stipulated amount of 20,000 INR was reached for a girl, her name was taken out from the broadcast.

Meanwhile Joy observed a bearded man frolicking around in the pandal in traditional bengali attire. He was looking like an Indian version of Santa Claus, giving away gifts and chocolates to everyone crossing him.

Joy was concerned, since if he is Nata Mallick's accomplice then he will use this goodwill to subsequently turn the crowd against him.

Though now he had realised that it needs a miracle for Shantipur to win the prize of the best Durga pujo, still he wanted to avoid any controversy or negative news.

He told Robi to quietly take the bearded man to an isolated place and see who he was because it was evident that the beard was artificial.

Robi went to the bearded person and hinted that on the other side of the pandal there are more children who are waiting for the chocolates.

As soon as the bearded man reached the other side, Robi toppled him down on the floor and pulled his beard.

Before he could ask further questions, he realised that his face looked very familiar. So he asked the man, 'What is your name?'

The bearded man responded, 'Kartik Bacchan.'

Robi got confused and thought he was joking, so he opined, 'And your father's name, is that famous star Rishi Bacchan?'

He responded, 'Yes.'

Subsequently, on the other side, Deep was frantically searching for Kartik Bacchan since he had envisaged that something like this might happen in Shantipur.

Deep followed the voice of Kartik to the other side of the pandal and saw Robi and his friends circled around Kartik. They were confused about finding such a superstar in their Durga pujo.

As they saw Deep, and it became clear to them that Deep had brought Kartik Bacchan to the Durga pujo.

Robi asked Deep, 'What are you doing here? Now, have you come on behalf of Nata Mallick to create a situation here?'

Deep heaved a sigh 'No my friend I have come to support our Durga pujo, we want us to win and that is the reason I have taken the favour from my friend and big star Kartik Bacchan to come here.'

Robi could not believe the words of Deep till Kartik himself explained how he cancelled the shooting of one of his film and flew to Kolkata on very short notice.

But Robi was still infuriated so he shouted at Deep to vent out his anger 'see what you have done with Pihu, she now has to raise a child single handedly while you are spending colourful nights with the actresses. Your small fun has resulted in a lifetime of struggle for her.'

Deep was calm, he had punished himself enough for this. He is a changed man now and mature enough to handle such situation.

Deep replied "I will talk to Pihu as well, this time. I have regretted enough for what I have done,but hope you know now that it was done in the fit of anger.

Meanwhile, Kartik Bacchan caught the attention of the media, and there was huge coverage fuelling rumours that the Bollywood actors were coming down to Shantipur to take part in the Durga pujo.

While the prime focus was the Durga pujo, the media was also covering different aspects arranged specially by Joy and his team in and around Durga pujo. The special sweet designed for the purpose of Durga pujo was a huge hit.

Sharad ensured that media coverage highlights the uniqueness of the Shantipur Durga Pujo and gets the attention of judges who were evaluating different Durga pujo.

Meanwhile Deep had to straighten things up with Pihu, so he decided to clarify the long pending misunderstanding with her.

He frantically searched for Pihu till he could find her with her daughter near a street food vendor. Her daughter was insisting on having a delicacy, and she rejected it.

Deep started moving toward Pihu, just then he saw Joy moving toward her. He felt for few second that time is again running out for him, again same frustration surfaced,like a déjà vu moment for him. But this time, he took hold of his emotion and took deep breaths. Just then Shree called Joy from other side to help her with some chore, and the path was clear for him to approach Pihu. When the time has come for some stories to complete, things fall in place.

Deep joined their discussion. 'Come on, such a cute girl deserves to get this delicacy; let Deep Uncle help you get the delicacy.'

Pihu was quiet and didn't speak a word, she was so scared that she was unable to speak, while Deep paid for the delicacy and told her daughter to share it with her friends.

Deep turned to Pihu "I can clearly see hate for me,while I look at you. You have clinched your fists in scare. Let me take two steps back to make you little comfortable. What I said that day about you and Joy was completely wrong but my intention of entering the ladies toilet was not malafide. I came after you to express my feelings about you and got puzzled when I saw Joy coming towards the school. Please forgive me if you can. I would like to complete what I couldn't, years back and that is to tell you that I still love you. I had been around many women but I have never loved anyone except you and I would be happy to spend rest of my life with you and our daughter.

Deep could clearly observe that the hardships of life have turned Pihu into a docile person. Now, she is a much quieter person than she used to be. The life in her has been sucked out by the nonchalant beatings of melancholic activities. She used to ask lots of questions in her school days, but now she has accepted that in life, you need to live with some unanswered questions.

Pihu was still quiet.

Tears started dripping from Deep's eyes.

Pihu responded now 'You have suffered more than enough, please relieve yourself from this burden, as I forgive you. I have started believing in destiny, so I believe that things would have turned out like this even if you had not done anything that day. So don't blame yourself for that.'

Deep wiped his tears. 'But I still have feelings for you; what do I do about that? Please give me a chance. I would love to take you and your daughter to Mumbai and start a new life together. Please don't treat this as a way to repent. It is a favour I am asking from you.'

Pihu didn't say anything; she just walked out without responding with yes or no.

Deep was perplexed, but he knew that he needed to focus his energy somewhere else.

Deep knew that before he can support Joy and his village, he needs to mend his relationship with Joy. Both of them were aware of the presence of each other, but they were trying to avoid each other. They didn't wanted the situation to go out of hand and turn into a quarrel between in front of the camera.

Deep thought of taking help of Sharad to get things straightened with Joy. Sharad called two of them in a room.

Sharad, as always made a short comment before closing the door after him "Joy, if you seek to be forgiven then you also need to forgive".

Deep spoke "I have made a big mistake that day by spreading a lie about you and Pihu on the last day of the school, but I had never imagined that it will take such a shape. Ultimately, I was punished equally for when I saw Pihu getting married off to a person ten years elder to her. To get over that guilt I resorted to alcohol, weeds and what not. However, I am a changed person now and I am willing to accept Pihu with her daughter. I know you also wish for the bright future of Pihu and her daughter. Lets get over old issues. I promise, I will not let you down.

Joy was touched by the comment of Sharad, because he realized that his friends will be observing as well, if he has the heart to forgive others as well, besides seeking to be forgiven.

Joy replied "Sometimes,whether we are able to forgive a person or not, depends on the price that we have paid for the mistake of that person. In this case, I feel rage whenever I see the struggles of Pihu. If Pihu forgives you then consider that I have forgiven you as well, if she doesn't forgive you then don't expect the forgiveness from me. I will not come in between you and Pihu. Let's see what course destiny takes.

Deep requested "Atleast then let me help with the Durga Puja arrangements, that way I will have a fair chance to convince Pihu.

Joy nodded Ok and then they both went out of the room.

Deep had also invited eminent singers from Bollywood for the cultural programme in the evening. The original plan was to again give chance to the homegrown talents to showcase their talents before the audience.

Deep tried to convince Joy to completely change the plan and had arranged for all the advanced musical equipments required for the performance by the celebrated singers, however Joy was very reluctant to budge as he believed that this would dilute the core purpose of the Durga pujo.

Ultimately, they agreed that the local singers would sing duets with the famous singers from Mumbai and the other special talents presenter with expertise in different domains would also present their skills in the intervals.

It was a huge hit with lots of cheers and dancing by the audience. It was a solace for the singers as well, as they always wanted their voice to reach rural India.

In the evening, Sandhi pujo was planned as per sequence. Sandhi pujo is performed to appease the warrior form of Goddess Durga i.e., Goddess Chamunda. The intention is to appreciate the valour of the warrior form of Maa Durga and imbibe those skills in our persona.

The significance of Sandhi pujo goes back to the times of Lord Rama, wherein it is said that he performed pujo with 108 lotuses to pray to Goddess Chamunda and seek her blessings in defeating the mighty Ravana. Following the same tradition, Sandhi pujo is performed at the juncture of the conclusion of the auspicious moment for Ashtami pujo and the beginning of the auspicious moment for Navami Pujo. At the end of Sandhi pujo, 108 lamps are offered to Goddess Chamunda as a symbolic offering to pray for family well-being and sound health.

Since we are praying the warrior form of Maa Durga, there is also tradition to sacrifice goats as an offering to Goddess Chamunda. Later the goat meat is cooked without any onion and ginger and distributed as a prasad.

This tradition has been going on for ages in Shantipur Durga Pujo as well when Joy's father Projoy Mukherjee was arranging the Durga pujo. However, Joy decided to deviate from age old tradition and decided to sacrifice raw papaya instead.

This created little ruckus amongst the people, as they misunderstood that Joy is trying to save money since vegetables are much cheaper than the goat meat.

Meanwhile, Nata Mallick had publicised that he would sacrifice 101 goats, and the meat would be distributed to all the visitors.

It was broadcasted on all the channels and Nata Mallick also came forward to explain the importance of sacrifice in Chamunda pujo and also criticised Joy for deviating from our traditions, but Joy didn't budge under the pressure of media, Nata Mallick and even his own few fellow villagers.

In Shantipur all the participants of the pujo had gathered memories of lifetime, many kids who had never seen a village life, got to see and experience it themselves. They saw how everything is not measured in terms of money in villages. Many times, they saw that they were given goodies without charging anything from them, just out of happiness that they took the timeout to visit their village.

It remains to be seen whether these aspects will be counted when the jury decides on the award for the best Durga pujo.

Navami

Navami Pujo of Durga Pujo celebrates the Mahishasura Mardini form of Maa Durga, which means the assassinator of the demon Mahishasura.

The legend goes that demon Mahishasura had evil interests on Maa Durga. After doing extreme penance he had attained blessings of supreme God that no man of God would be able to kill him. After receiving such power, he started wreaking havoc on the people of all three paradigms and also started misbehaving with women.

At such a juncture, he got to know that the wife of Lord Shiva, i.e., Goddess Durga, is very beautiful. He thought in his mind that since any man could not kill me, I could misbehave with Goddess Durga, and she would not be saved by anyone.

Little did he know that women who give birth to a baby are far stronger than men when the situation arises.

He entered the dwelling place of Maa Durga hiding inside a buffalo, but as soon as he tried to come out and misbehave with her, she turned to her supreme self with ten hands all equipped with swords.

Fierce battle ensued between Maa Durga and Mahishasura, which ultimately ended with Maa Durga piercing her trisula (trident) into the Chest of Mahishasura.

Pandit babu had started the pujo early in the morning. All the disciples were now habituated to this new healthier lifestyle. There are around six big ponds in and around Shantipur, so special bathing arrangements were made for all the visitors to experience community bathing as still prevalent in rural India.

Everyone was ready on time to offer flowers to Maa Durga. There was mixed feeling in the hearts of people since tomorrow would be the last day of Durga pujo, and then they would have to wait again for a whole year for such festivities.

Competitions were arranged in sidelines to encourage participation of people such as conch shell blowing competition, balancing the bamboo sticks on forehead, spell bees and tongue twisters.

Deep has not touched on the topic of marriage with Pihu again but he took the opportunity to spend as much time as possible with her daughter.

Deep and Pihu also helped Pandit Babu with pujo arrangements. Deep could sense that the hatred visible in the eyes of Pihu had vanished now. Deep also met Pihu's mother to apologize for the misdeed he did in the school and also mentioned his desire to take all of them to Mumbai with them. Deep realized that he had mentioned Pihu to take her and her daughter Ruchi, but he was not aware of that Pihu's mother is also alive. He needs to make that clear to her that he meant all of them.

Shree had arranged for the collection of all the flowers and biodegradable materials used in Durga pujo to be converted into biofertilisers. She had also involved small children in making these arrangements. Plastic overuse has turned into a menace now, and Shree very well knew that if we don't stop the overuse of plastic, then we are unknowingly preparing for our extinction. She engaged locals to prepare plates and glasses from banana leaves that are abundantly available in the area. Poster competitions were arranged where children sensitised the people on the issue of non-biodegradable wastes.

Very soon, the results of the best Durga pujo for this year will be out on television. Praful Mukherjee, the uncle of Joy Mukherjee, was happy beyond limits to have spent such a quality time with the whole family after decades.

Many residents of Shantipur who had migrated to other states and cities in search of better opportunities were proud beyond limits, and they decided to come see the Durga pujo next year.

Meanwhile, Nata Mallick used all his diplomatic powers to try his best to influence the jury.

At 7 pm, the results for the best Durga pujo were declared, and Durga Pujo of Nata Mallick was declared as the best Durga pujo. Nata Mallick was all over the media, giving interviews.

However, there was a special mention of Shantipur Durga pujo because of the unique decoration concepts done by them, the social awareness they have created and the unique concept they have launched.

Here in Shantipur, people were feeling dejected by this news as they firmly believed there was a chance for them to win the award of the best Durga pujo.

Some visitors decided to return to their home early because they had anchored all their joy and happiness with the fact of being associated with the winning team.

Sharad tried to find the reason for such a result and learned that it was politically influenced by Nata Mallick.

Joy could sense the dip in the energy level of the people, so they organised a Dunuchi dance competition in the evening at very short notice. It is a devotional dance to adore Maa Durga with a fire made of coconut shreds on a metal bowl.

It is performed with the background music of Dakhi and creates a divine environment.

Everyone performed the Dunuchi dance with great fervour, it was so consuming that it gave an opportunity to everyone to forget the recent setback.

When everyone was completely exhausted and were served with local lemon drink, suddenly there was a voice coming from the speaker 'I knew from the very beginning that we would not win the best Durga pujo.'

All the heads rolled towards the direction of the sound to see who it was, and it was Joy.

Joy continued, 'I knew from the beginning that it is nearly impossible for us to win the award of the best Durga pujo, not because we are not capable but because we all know that such awards are highly influenced by many forces who have their own vested interests. But still, I took this challenge because when we take on a task greater than our capability, in the process, we become a better version of ourselves. We regain trust in our capabilities, we find new opportunities, make new friends, new beginnings ...so many things. For me, this Durga pujo is a huge success, and to celebrate our success, let hail Maa Durga ...Joy Maa Durga!!!! And the whole crowd reverted with a huge shout, 'Joy Maa Durga.'

Everyone was re-energised. They were hugging and appreciating each other.

Just then one media person covering the Durga pujo, comes to Joy and his team with the latest news that the Government of West Bengal has decided that they will not allow any Durga pujo association to take out the procession of Maa Durga since there will be celebration of Muharram by Muslim Community on the same day.

Muharram is the first month of the Islamic calendar and they take out processions on the last day to mourn the death of Imam Hussain ibn Ali, the grandson of Prophet Mohammed.

Evidently, the government has taken this political decision to influence and get the Muslim votes in the upcoming elections. However, when you are responsible for the well-being of 100 million people, you need to take some hard measures to maintain law and order. Nobody wants to make hard decisions; however, sometimes life doesn't give you any options.

Two bad news in a single day, left Joy full of anger and frustration. All the gratitude towards Rasulpur village and the thought of communal harmony has disappeared. The animal instinct of fight or flight has taken over the Shantipur village.

It is to be seen how this incident influences the remaining part of the story, since this is not the last chapter.

Vijayadashami

Vijayadashami is a Sanskrit word which translates into 'Victorious tenth day.' This is so because on this day, the incarnation of Lord Vishnu, Rama had restored the balance in the society by killing demon Ravana.

This is also the day when all the concluding prayers are done to Maa Durga and her clay statue is immersed in water with silent pledge of Durga pujo celebration the coming year.

This also symbolises Maa Durga's return to her home in Mount Kailash to stay with Lord Shiva.

Traditionally sweets are offered to Maa Durga and her entourage. All the married women put vermillion on Maa Durga forehead, which is a symbol of married woman, and on each other. This is a symbolic celebration of womanhood.

Once all the concluding prayers are done, the procession of Maa Durga is taken to the bank of a river or pond and immersed there.

The Durga pujo ends with dispersion of Shanti Jal on all the devotees. This is considered as blessings of Maa Durga and it is believed that it would keep them healthy, peaceful, and prosperous.

Here in Shantipur, everyone was in a state of thoughtlessness. It had been a normal tradition to conclude the Durga pujo with the immersion of the Durga idol, but now they are being compelled to postpone this joy.

Nata Mallik had tried all his vices to find a workaround so that he can immerse the idol of his Durga pujo, but he had to pay the price for being a celebrity. In such situations the noose is tightened more on well-known people to set an example.

Joy was also filled with anguish for the Muslim community. He was feeling betrayed as he ensured that they also benefited from the Durga pujo celebration, and now, because of them, he will be unable to immerse the Maa Durga idol.

It is very common for all of us to blame the people closer to us than the actual person who has caused the damage sitting at a distant place because we also know we can do no harm to the distant person, and that is exactly what Joy was engrossed in.

Sharad, being an editor, had also tried everything to see if he could arrange for a special permit to immerse Maa Durga idol.

The police force was stationed in all the Durga pujo to ensure compliance with the protocol.

Robi and Moloy were not that sad because they have made a bumper business because of Durga pujo. The videos of Moloy weaving factory had been uploaded in Youtube and had received many likes. It was surprising for everyone to notice that you can earn money out of uploading videos.

Shree has not been keeping well since last night. She had been vomiting frequently.

All the visitors had started returning to their homes from last night except a few who thought of staying one more day to enjoy the delicacies.

Maa was satisfied, as she could attend Durga pujo in Shantipur after ages, meet old friends, and cherish old memories.

Pihu has rejuvenated. It has infused a new life in her. She had again turned into the jovial Pihu. This is the reason everyone should have a hobby because that keeps you alive.

Deep was full of hope. He met Pihu and reinstated his desire to marry her and take her, Ruchi and her mother with him to Mumbai.

Panditbabu was thankful to Maa Durga as alliances started flowing in for his daughter when he was featured on television explaining the importance and meaning of Durga pujo. It is evident now that her beauty was never the real reason, but her position in the social hierarchy. Panditbabu was praying for this kind of celebration every year.

Everyone was doing their work silently as if they were in a state of half-sleep. As if they were trying to withhold a storm within them.

But like everything in life, even storms are inevitable when it is their time to come.

Suddenly, everyone saw a huge crowd of Muslims coming towards them.Some people started murmuring that they were coming here to mock us by showing their processions.

Some young people started gathering sticks to beat them up if they mocked us.

There was so much rage in people that the situation could turn into a communal riot at any time.

Joy was also taken over by the rage because of the inability to immerse the Maa Durga idol.

It is surprising to observe how people can quickly turn against each other, with the slightest instigation, while claiming to be best friends.

Maa looked at the developments from the façade and immediately came to the front, taking Piku in her lap.

She was an intelligent woman, and she did this to ensure some time to gauge the situation, as nobody will start fighting if there is a chance of hurting a small children.

Maa commands everyone in a strong tone: 'Nobody will go out; only I will talk to them first.'

Shree also came forward, 'I will also stay with you, Maa.'

Maa pointed towards the crowd. 'Everyone keeps your sticks behind; I don't want to see any of them.

Soon, the crowd of Muslims came near, and they could see Muhammad Rehman leading them.

The crowd stopped before Maa, police constables stationed there to avoid the immersion of the Maa Durga idol eloped, expecting communal violence. They pragmatically thought that two constables could not stop anything, so it was better to save our lives.

Muhammad Rehman said 'Memsahib, we are deeply saddened by the decision of our government to stop the immersion of Durga pujo and we feel that it is unwise on the part of the government to stop either party to celebrate their festival in communal harmony. Let us all take Maa Durga to the bank of the river and immerse it jointly.'

'We all have benefited from this Durga pujo celebration, and we would all pray that it happens with the same fervour every year.'

It had been the longest sentence Mohammad Rehman had ever spoken, considering his introverted nature.

Maa was touched by this gesture, and she understood that if Maa Durga's idols need to be immersed, it needs to be done before the two constables come back with reinforcements.

Maa exclaimed, 'then, without further delay, let's lift Maa Durga together and take it to the bank of river Ganga.'

So, with the huge hailing of 'Bolo bolo Durga Mai Ki,' they all hauled Maa Durga on a truck and took it to the bank of the river Ganga.

The communal harmony was back, as now Hindus and Muslims were hugging each other, sharing sweets, and applying colours playfully on each other.

There was a sense of achievement and accomplishment in all.

Jointly, they successfully immersed Maa Durga into the Ganga River and prayed for her arrival again next year.

Maa, Shree, and Piku also went to the bank of the river to witness that.

Once immersion was done with huge pomp and show, Maa turned to Shree.

Maa smiled. 'My girl, do you want to give me any good news?'

Shree was blushing. 'How do you know?'

Maa playfully replied, 'In our times, there were no testing kits for pregnancy, so we used to guess by observing the change in the women.'

They hugged each other. It will be a long time since the house was filled with baby cries.

Pihu realised that she had come to the bank of the river holding Deep's hand throughout.

Deep had been holding her on one hand and her daughter on another hand. There was distance and there was closeness at the same time. Both have suffered enough. Maybe now destiny wants to give them their share of happiness.

Deep realised that Pihu didn't have the strength to say either yes or no. She needed unconditional support right now. So, he just whispered in Pihu's ears, 'You are mine now,' and pulled her closer to him. She rested her head on his shoulder as a sign of silent acceptance. In every generation, you will find couples who have never expressed their love to each other in words but many times through gestures. Deep had this moment to say I love you to Pihu; instead, he decided to own her completely with her qualities and faults.

When everything comes to consummation, how can we forget Nata Mallick?

To avenge the denial of permission to immerse Maa Durga idol, he decided to give an advertisement in the front page of the newspaper specifying the time of immersion of the Maa Durga idol the next day and mentioned that all the attendees will get a packet of sweet as a good gesture.

He had chosen Sharad's newspaper so as to rebuke him further for contributing to Shantipur 's Durga pujo.

So late in the evening, after Sharad had returned from the bank of the river immersing Maa Durga idol, he received a call from promoters of the newspaper informing that he needed to make necessary changes in the first page for including this advertisement.

Sharad was waiting for this moment for ages, so he informed that he would make the required space. He sat the whole night to write another article on Shantipur' s Durga pujo and included that article just besides Nata Mallick's advertisement.

So, the next day, Nata Mallick's world turned upside down when he saw the front page of the newspaper.

On the left side of the page, there was his advertisement on immersion of his Maa Durga idol later that day and just besides that there was an article with heading 'The real best Durga pujo spreading communal harmony in the plural society.' There was a picture of Hindus and Muslims taking Maa Durga idol together to the bank of river for immersion.

He complained to the authorities how this was done. There was outrage in the media by political representatives against such a gesture. But in the heart of the people, everyone knew that this is exactly what Durga pujo is all about.

It is about celebrating the differences, celebrating the togetherness after bereavement for a long year, celebrating the homecoming of the girl of the house.

Durga pujo is not only about spending huge amounts of money to create huge pandals and huge Durga Maa idols. It is about having that long pending talk with our near and dear ones over a cup of tea and some cutlets. Some slowness in life, listening to the Rabindra sangeet, taking out old family photo albums and watching them together, taking dust out of that old guitar and playing some old familiar tunes on it.

This Durga pujo has ushered in new life for the different characters in the story and also maybe a new perspective.

Joy could see pride in the eyes of Misti when she talks about her experiences in India with her friends. Her stories are never ending and full of exclamations and expressions.

Joy and Shree are expecting their second child and they are thinking that his journey practically started with an exceptional Durga pujo.

Maybe next year, Nata Mallick will also travel to Shantipur to enjoy Durga pujo. Maa, Joy, Shree, and Misti will come again from Denmark, and Pihu, Deep, and Ruchi will come from Mumbai. Sharad would come with new advertising suggestions, Moloy will get another chance to express his creativity, Robi will develop another flavour of sweet dessert specially for the Durga Pujo.

Maybe many new people will join next year's Durga pujo after the success of this year, many new stories will emerge from there, many new beginnings will be set into motion, and many pleasantries will be exchanged.

There are so many possibilities, but it would not be the same. No two events in life are the same and that makes every moment of life worth enjoying to the fullest.

So, while different characters in the story start their new life, I leave this moment for you to sit alone and relive similar memories from the past or plan such an event in the future.

May the blessings of Maa Durga be with all of you.

Joy Maa Durga

Background

I started writing this story in 2016, just out of an idea that came to my mind when I moved to Denmark from India. It took me eight years to complete this book just because I never forced myself to finish the book. I waited for different events to happen, inspiration to come so that I could make it part of this book. I had written the pages of the book sometimes at night, sometimes at the airport, and sometimes while on vacation, but only when I really felt like writing and adding to this book.

In the course of this eight years so many interesting things have happened. I have been blessed with a son (who will later question me 'why Joy Mukherjee does not have a son') and also interestingly as the law of attraction goes, in 2019, I was part of six families that started community Durga pujo outside Copenhagen in Denmark for the first time. I was the priest for the Durga pujo without any prior experience.

You are welcome to go through the Facebook page of 'Bengali's in Aalborg' to connect real images with some of the portions of the story.

This book is not only for the Bengalis. While reading the book, you should be reminded of your own childhood memories and of your struggle to keep your culture alive outside India, irrespective of which part of the country you belong to.

We live in a diverse world. We all have different faces, languages, culture, and way of life but all our heartbeats sound the same. I am hopeful that while reading this book you will reconnect with your childhood memories, incidences, friendships, and stories and will find the time you have invested in reading this book, enjoyable and relaxing.